WHAT'S MY SECRET?

What's My Secret?

Lesley-Madeleine

ATHENA PRESS
LONDON

ISBN: 978 1 84748 254 9

First published 2008 by
ATHENA PRESS
Queen's House, 2 Holly Road
Twickenham TW1 4EG
United Kingdom

Some of the names in this book have been changed in order to
protect and maintain the privacy of others.

Printed for Athena Press

Order of Addresses Where We Resided

Elmwood, Homestead Road, Chelsfield	b. Sept 1942
Manor House, Newlands, Sherborne, Dorset	June 1943
6 Beblets Cotts, Worlds End Lane, Green St. Green, Farnborough, Kent	Feb 1944
Primrose Cottage, Sherborne, Dorset	March 1944
Waldens, St. Mary Cray, Kent	July 1946
Goda Road, Littlehampton, Sussex	Oct 1946
St. Mary Cray, Kent	— 1954
Bromley, Kent	— 1956
I left School	1957

Contents

FOREWORD

In January 2006, a northern bottlenose whale swam up the Thames in London attracting worldwide attention. Amazingly, a deep-sea creature had ventured far out of its territory and made its way right up to the Houses of Parliament, almost as if requesting an audience or acting as an emissary, one might think.

The seven-ton, eighteen-foot mammal needed, for its safety, to turn around and go back to its source, but it was disorientated. So much so, that this could not be achieved.

I identify with the need to go back to one's beginnings but I am also disorientated. When people try to help me, like they tried to help the whale, reaching out to touch me, they harm me just like they harmed it. If I go forward I, like it, become increasingly distressed in an alien environment. I have had what may have been considered expert care of late, but just like the bottlenose I may have to give up if my treatment is incorrect.

There are deep layers of snow in my heart as I look out of the window this springtime and see the disliked Bullfinch busy on the prunus. This is my first sighting of him this March. I think of how he is spurned, not for his own fault but because of his tendency to nip fruit trees in the bud. I am convinced that I have been stunted because my mother and I were compelled to live in six different places for the first four years of my life and that was just the beginning.

The bird I watch is bright and admirable, just as my mother was in my eyes, but she mirrored him in the fact that she had made enemies, rightly or wrongly, because of the fact that, in 1939, England was visited by what was commonly termed 'the Canadian problem'.

She fell hopelessly into the arms of one of these visitors; a single girl's dream come true. Just as the Bullfinches invade the trees, the Canadians invaded our women, so it is said, thus the fruit growers complain bitterly about the bird, and society victimised unmarried mothers for spoiling England's reputation. Those loose women, who came under the spell of the enthusiastic men who partied and romanced them, being considered oversexed and over here, were slighted. The British men were away at war leaving us undefended, but Canadians arrived on our shore and there were clearly more men than we knew what to do with.

Sadly the sins, although they are no longer so considered, are visited upon the children, and I in my turn felt like a cuckoo dumped in the nest of other breeds – many families where I was placed while Mother went out to work when I was a babe, toddler and young child. She left me silently grief-stricken behind her. In some cases the offspring of the households made no secret of their dislike of me, rushing to blame me, the outsider, when things went wrong. One admitted unashamedly when I met her in adult life that she had disliked me for being held up as an example of perfection, little did she realise that in my position there was no choice. It was made clear by Mother that I should always be on my guard and behave properly in other people's homes so as not to give them any reason to turn us out.

Being like the Bullfinch I was deprived of protection in most areas. The British Press caused us to become known as the 'war children', a mild term for what was considered the result of a dishonourable liaison between British women and Canadian soldiers.

The bird, *Pyrrhula pyrrhula*, encroaches when his natural food becomes scarce. I did whatever I did through lack of natural love and attention. Retiring from human presence because of shyness, mistrust and inability to understand correct interactions, just like my buddy, the Bullfinch. I call him such because the animal kingdom has been my mainstay throughout life. With nothing concrete to hold onto, I have found dumb creatures to be ever-present helpers in some form, assisting me to get by. They will appear in different shapes throughout my story.

I believe strongly in one concept now and that is that hindrances are placed in our way in order to test us and prove that we are strong enough to transcend them. They also add purpose. The aid of my animal friends and a firm faith that there is always hope over the horizon enabled me to come this far. There is however, under this now 'resolute rock', a lurking and grave, freshly uncovered secret for me to deal with.

What's my secret? Read on and find out.

IN SEARCH OF THE CHURCH OF MY BAPTISM

It is not easy for me to decide where to begin the story of my journey. However, if I do not take this chance to tell it, I will always regret it. My motive for this has never been recognition. It is purely for release and self-healing of unresolved mental and emotional blocks from my strange, inhibited past life, which was full of taboos until 1996, when my mother died, and further discoveries were made in 1999.

I cannot believe how such obvious questions I should have asked my mother remained repressed and unassuaged until it was too late.

When I started my search, Mother's tattered WWII ID card held most of the clues for the discovery of my early lost childhood. The card was pale green with the entries written in blue fountain pen and official registration date stamps. It listed five places of residence for my mother between June 1943 and October 1946.

The story of my search will therefore begin with the short episode of my hunt for the second location listed on Mother's ID card. It was in this area that I was baptised, so I went to look for the church of my baptism near our place of residence at that time. This was an obvious place to start, especially as the ID card offered no clues as to the place of my birth in 1942.

This search, conducted on Sunday, 12 March 2006, became a most surprising outing following my usual reticent start at 2 p.m. I retard the times of departure to find these places for some unknown reason buried in my subconscious, but as constantly proves the case I end up pleasantly elated.

My husband, Robert, and I targeted the area of Green Street Green, near the village of Chelsfield, Orpington, Kent. It was a Sunday afternoon and we didn't want to go far due to limited time and the possibility of heavy traffic. We headed therefore for the second place on my mother's ID card where she is noted to have stayed in 1944. It was 6 Beblets Cottages, Worlds End Lane, (what a wonderful name, I would return to photograph the sign later, in case nobody would believe me), Green Street Green.

We had no idea where the church of my baptism was as it did not appear on the map obtained from a website. On searching Worlds End Lane, which seemed to go on forever so we could easily imagine how it got its name, we suddenly came upon the church whilst screwing our necks round in every direction trying to read numbers and names on every possible house or cottage looking for 'Beblets Cottages'. One end had been totally taken over by high-society mansions of new design, quite incredible in this unsuspected area, and most were protected by huge iron gates and security systems. When we first spotted the church, Robert commented that it wasn't much to look at, but I could warmly view it with eyes of one who might have seen it erected in 1937. The building was sandstone and in a few places amongst the mainly dirty stones we could see replacement stones, which looked so clean and bright, and such a lovely colour. I imagined the whole building as being like this originally, containing big, blank, windows and letting in a lot of light. The inside, though unobtainable as we were locked out, could be viewed through the door and was similarly disappointing. Quite drab and not at all as I'd like to see a house of God. Nevertheless we had found it, and although I felt impelled to inspire the neighbourhood to pull together with gusto and give it a thoroughly good spring clean – that is until I remembered the red tape of today which would prevent even one of us approaching a ladder – I was glad to have come upon it, and to have put another piece into my jigsaw. We continued our quest for the cottages after taking relevant photos. We proved to be unsuccessful in this, but did not go home empty-handed, so to speak.

The tracking device we used to find the church was my baptism card. I am very fond of the picture on it. It is a scene of an engrossed crowd in gowns of red, yellow and blue. The throng is gathered around Jesus, who is holding an infant on his lap in the crook of his right arm, whilst he issues a blessing to another with his left hand. There are yellow, undulating sand dunes in the background. It is colourful and reminds me of how difficult it was in those times – 25 October 1942 – to achieve the feat of baptism, when the first named sponsor was an unmarried mother with her babe in arms – the dreaded illegitimate! I am thankful to her for my baptism and the fact that while most babies like me were given up for adoption, I was not – although she threatened me with it often when angry and I was much older.

My birthday was 8 September 1942, the church of baptism was Saint Mary's and quite coincidentally, Our Lady's birthdate was the same as mine or, more correctly, mine as hers. I feel humbled by this comforting factor. Another remarkable fact is that I am married to a man whose birth day is Christmas Day, the same date as Jesus Christ. Wow, what a connection! I hope I am not being presumptuous about stating this.

On Tuesday, 14 March we are to hunt for the remaining sponsors, Mr and Mrs Parrott.

AMETHYST INCIDENT

We stopped to take a photograph of the signpost saying Worlds End Lane en route to St Mary Cray, Orpington, Kent where we hoped to find the fourth place recorded on Mothers' ID card for the year 1946. It was a rainy day and I was dispirited. As Robert struggled to park our red Mini Cooper on the blind bend of the road, I was thinking that he and the camera were going to get very wet and we were only at the start of our day.

Continuing to St Mary Cray, we passed places that I remembered well as we had gone back to the area to live again many years later, which I will tell of in due course.

We discovered our objective, Waldens Road, then traversed back and forth seemingly endlessly until running out of hope; we stopped outside a garden nursery for help. Robert got out and beckoned a man and woman from behind their locked gate to ask what they knew of the area. I was tired by this time and waited in the car, but Robert returned saying that the old manor was right next to us up a private road. There were warning signs against our approach which had previously impeded us, but we were told not to heed them. We would find Waldens Manor, with Little (modern) Waldens beside it. They advised us to go and speak to the lady who resided in the building of our interest. Our helpers had said they were certain she would be pleased to tell us its history.

Nervously we ventured along the narrow lane, as I am

always wary of guard dogs or angry farmers. We found a fork in the road and, choosing to explore the right limb, found that this part led to a waste tip, so we backed up and took the left. We discovered Little Waldens at the bottom of the lane and then on our way back out, spotted, concealed behind trees and bushes, an enormous old manor which formerly was out of our view. It was lovely to behold. This had to be what we were looking for. We got out of the vehicle to get a closer look, but the place name was eroded from the wooden mount and we daren't venture further even though there was a car in the drive for fear of disturbing people unannounced. The next day I was to write an appealing letter:

15 March 2006

Dear Sarah,

We came to find your property yesterday and, after speaking to the people at the garden nursery, managed to catch a glimpse of it.

My interest in it is that my deceased mother has the name Waldens on her ID card. We are assuming it was your manor as these are the type of places where she frequently worked. I am a war baby and she had many addresses where she worked or stayed, trying to keep me with her, following September 1942 when I was born, and I am trying to piece the bits together. She was at your address in 1946, her name was Margaret E Steer.

The people at the garden nursery said to ask you about the history, but I did not like to disturb you unannounced as I thought my husband and I could frighten you, although a car was parked outside your lovely house and we were very tempted.

One place where I stayed with her, the people were called 'Parrott', and they had three little goats in those days. She stayed at five places by the end of 1946 so it may not have been at your address. They in fact became my god-

18

parents or sponsors on my baptism card. I would love to know of them. I was baptised at St Mary's Church, Green Street Green in October 1942, and have just found where that is.

If you can write and tell me anything I'd be grateful. Maybe a small photo of the house for my research album or book, as I have found my fathers' Canadian family after mothers' death in 1996, having to wait so as not to upset her. She went through such a lot to keep me. She said one family wanted to adopt me but I don't know who they are either. I'm telling you this in case you are interested as most people are, in the story.

Thanking you in anticipation of hearing from you and hoping not to cause you any inconvenience.

Yours sincerely,

Lesley-Madeleine.

I never had a response from this lady or managed to track the Parrotts and was very puzzled and disappointed. A possible explanation for this could be a piece of information I later received, revealing that Sarah was apparently in a dispute with some people who wanted to buy her land, and had subsequently become very wary of strangers. However, I cannot verify the truth of this.

*

After finishing with the area of St Mary Cray we went back via Chelsfield village and stopped for a comfort break. Robert said that if we had blinked we would have missed the village. We asked some men drinking in the pub whether they were locals and how we could find out what had happened to the cottages in Worlds End Lane. They confirmed that they knew the district and directed us to Bromley Civic Centre where records of such things are kept. We were now pushed for time as it was mid-afternoon and we had no idea as to when these offices would be shut. Arriving in Bromley however, it couldn't have been easier. We parked at the multi-storey with ease and to our left as we came onto the street were the buildings we sought. The traffic is usually manic here so this was a stroke of luck. We first homed in on the planning section where again the help was impeccable. We were assured by a pleasant lady, after giving details of the cottages and where we could be reached, that she would contact us quite quickly.

We had been told on our arrival that the registrar's office would be closing shortly but we had chosen to opt for the cottage locating first. Now we got a speed up and climbed the stairs of an adjacent building where I, with uncontrolled shaky voice, explained with excitement to the registrar how crucial it was for me to obtain a full birth certificate with me and mother on it together and, as an added bonus, even find a record of my actual birth address in Chelsfield, Kent. The lady examined what I had in my possession very coolly and informed me that it was only a 'receipt' of my birth; that hurt. Then I showed her something else which my mother got for me when I was fifteen and she flatly said that that was only a 'short' birth certificate – short to me meant that yet again I'd been short-changed. However, she took that piece of evidence and proceeded to find out what she could about my place of birth (whilst I sat and attempted to fill in those forms we all dread), and if she could, she added, she would provide me with a full certificate, to which I replied that it would mean so much to me.

It was with a joyous spirit that I eventually read the pre-sented full birth certificate, it had all seemed too easy but at last at the age of sixty-three years old I had in my hands what most other people have in their possession with never a second thought from the date of their birth. I thanked the lady quite profusely. She did show slight emotion then, but was still rather reserved compared to another registrar I had met in my home town register office, who requested that I keep her informed of my progress. I discovered then that I had yet to apply to gain my father's name on my certificate. Maybe the superintendent registrar at Bromley had thought it would appear unprofessional to show too much interest and enthusiasm, or maybe she needed to contrast my intense mood, or perhaps it was neither and she just took these things in her stride.

I didn't want her to fold this treasure, so she gracefully proffered a second, bigger envelope and I slid it in carefully, frightened of touching it! Returning to the car we were a little dazed after a long, draining day and, at 6 p.m., we drove in to a Harvester restaurant in Southborough, Kent, to avoid the accumulating traffic, not caring much what we ate, but truly satisfied with our day.

What follows is a rendition of the planning departments' findings that I received by email the next day as promised:

Dear Lesley,

With reference to your visit to planning reception at the Civic Centre, Bromley on 14 March 2006, I can tell you that Worlds End Lane was renumbered in 1971. 6 Beblets Cottages was renumbered 114 Worlds End Lane, Orpington. I do not have your current address but if you would like a copy of the street naming and numbering certificate please contact me.

I hope this information is of help in your research.

Yours sincerely,

Jean Connelly

Of course, by the time I received the above reply regarding Beblets where I thought I may have been born, I had newly discovered my proper place of birth from the Civic Centre as being 'Elmwood', Homestead Road in Chelsfield.[*] I immediately turned the email around, replying to sender with an appeal for one more favour – that she attempt to find this site – which we had only been able to pinpoint regarding the road on our way home from Bromley Civic Centre, even after making several requests for this information from passers-by on the street, thus ending this particular chase in vain. I received the following reply:

7 April 2006

Dear Mrs Fenner,

Your enquiry has been forwarded to us. I have found Elmwood in the electoral registers of 1838–9 and 1939–40, in Green Street Green ward. The occupiers were Hector Le Provost and his wife Alice Munro le Provost. No one else is listed there, which suggests it was a private house, not an institution with resident staff. All the houses in Homestead Road had names, not numbers, which makes identification in later years difficult. I can't find it in the register for 1950, the first we have after the war. It may have been renamed 'Upways', but the occupier has changed (Alice A Kidd) and the arrangement of the houses is slightly different, so I cannot be sure.

I hope this helps you,

Yours sincerely,
Elizabeth Silverthorn
Archivist

I had begun to think I was born in an institute!
I noted with interest the reference on the birth certificate

---

[*] Elmwood, Chelsfield and Green Street Green all come under Orpington, formerly Farnborough.

to Mother being a domestic servant because I think it would be quite rare in these days to refer to someone in this manner. I think maybe she didn't want me to see that. I believe that nowadays most job titles have been altered to appear more agreeable. Personally I have no problem with this term but I suspect Mother may have had in later days in this role.

It seems appropriate to state here that my mother's birth certificate reads Maggie Etheline Steer and, knowing her as I do, she obviously thought the name Margaret more appealing to the circles she would work in. I only found that she was Maggie when she died and I received her documents.

In the later months of 1946 Mother took me to Littlehampton in Sussex and we encountered Commander Kerans and his wife and daughter. I played with Charmian Kerans for many happy hours and think of her fondly as she was such a sweet little girl. It is interestingly one of the longest periods I stayed in one place during my formative years where Mother acted as housekeeper for Mrs Searle. When I come to that year and its happenings I will recount it more fully. Charmian made me a charming little bookmark. It's of typical bookmark size and has on it a large guardian angel with vast yellow wings and a purple robe. It is looming over and blessing with outstretched hands a kneeling child in a blue gown, whose head is buried in its hands in prayer. It is surrounded by a green border, which also contains the words 'He shall give His Angels charge concerning thee'. She coloured it in and signed it for me and I have kept it close all these years to remind me of my particular guardian angel.

Charmian's father sailed down the Yangtze River in 1949, when I would have been seven. While involved in the Chinese civil war, his allotted ship was called the HMS *Amethyst*.

The United Kingdom kept a warship on the Yangtze River at Nanjing. On 20 April (the date of my first wedding anniversary years later) the *Amethyst* came under attack. During ensuing activity the ship became grounded on Rose Island when under heavy fire. It was full of gaping holes which had to be repeatedly plugged with anything suitable the crew could get their hands on.

HMS *Consort* tried to rescue her in vain. *Amethyst* was only retrieved from the mud on 26 April, by then very short on supplies.

On 30 July 1949 the *Amethyst*, under Commander Kerans' direction, slipped her chains at night and headed down river. In trepidation of being shot at by guns on each bank if spotted by searchlights playing on the water, she managed fortuitously to evade them and eventually reached the mouth of the river and freedom. Commander Kerans was played by Richard Todd in the film of 1957 which re-enacts this story.

Mum elaborated on the story of the ship's cat, Simon, a tale which always interested me. They used to allow cats on board – firstly to act as pest control and also because they were welcome companions for those away from home on the open sea. Eventually it was forbidden for hygienic reasons, but Seaman Hickinbottom smuggled Simon aboard, much to the other seamen's delight I'm sure. The cat duly became accepted and repaid its new friends by being a regular and expert rat catcher. Mother told me he was nicknamed Blackie and that he would have been a great comfort to the men. Unfortunately, he sustained injuries when they were under fire, so they undoubtedly licked their wounds together.

After the *Amethyst*'s courageous dash, Simon was given the equivalent to our VC. It was called the Dickin Medal and obviously made him famous. Sadly, Simon became ill when quarantined and shut away from his friends. He then gave up the ghost and, following this, was buried at Ilford's animal cemetery. There are many websites charting this well-known story with more details than I have been given.

I feel it is nice to end on this more romantic note, showing that life as the daughter of a domestic servant was not always dull, even though we were confined to servant's quarters and slept in one room, sharing a bed. I have met interesting people and have heard stories of varied lives and I do not regret that.

Initial Request for an Amendment to New Full Birth Certificate

Originally I had emailed a government body which seemed to have replaced Somerset House, London, well known for dealing with registrations of births, deaths and marriages in England and Wales, and they had directed me to a solicitor.

28 February 2006

Dear Mrs Fenner,

Under English law, if the natural parents of a child are not married to each other, the father's details can only be recorded in the birth register if both parents attend together.

As both your mother and father have passed away, your only option now is to petition the courts for a 'declaration of parentage'.

We cannot say what evidence the court may need to see when considering your request, but suggest you seek the advice of a solicitor who specialises in Family Law matters.

The solicitor I approached sent me to a register office, so I chose the nearest to begin with in my town of Crowborough, East Sussex, which I visited on 9 March 2006.

I told them that I wished to have my father's name added to my birth certificate along with my mother's and mine. I was informed in a kindly manner that I had only a registration of my birth at the time, and upon reaching fifteen years old had only received a short certificate – this I already knew. Consequently it was deemed advisable for me to contact the county court in Tunbridge Wells, Kent in order to petition the courts for a declaration of parentage, under Section 55A (1) of Family Law Act 1986, because neither of my parents were alive to vouch for me. This confirmed the advice I had received from my solicitor who had done a little research for me and usefully given me the extra information that I could probably do this myself and save money.

However, having returned home and immediately ringing Tunbridge Wells Court, they set me even further adrift it seemed, by saying I needed to apply to a magistrate's court. We decided our best option was to try Maidstone, Kent. We planned this trip for 16 March.

While I lay in bed on the fateful Thursday at 7.30 a.m. with my start-of-the-day cup of tea, my friend the Bullfinch ardently attacked the prunus again, working along the boughs little by little, accompanied by his faded counterpart, as is their wont for that time of the year. It is with amusement that I reflect on how I am eating away at the chains that bind me one bit at a time. Indeed throughout my lifetime I have done this tirelessly. Robert had arranged things so that we could set off at 11 a.m. and head straight for the multi-storey car park in Maidstone. It was very full. The traffic near the town had appeared daunting, but we made it and after going up several floors we at last squeezed into one empty space. The alarm in the adjacent car decided to go off and I hoped that this was not to be a bad omen. We had decided that we would go and eat first as it was lunchtime and then we could put all our attention into the pressing errand. The walk to the magistrate's court was easy after only one wrong turn. We checked in our personal belongings then waited at reception. We were asked what our mission was and then a telephone call was made to a department upstairs which we were then directed to. We ascended and, on explaining my reason for being there, the young lady in charge said she needed to refer us to a higher official as this was an unusual case. We waited with bated breath. An older lady with a pleasant face came out of another office and asked me to repeat my cause which I dutifully did, 'After all this time,' she exclaimed, whilst starting to look over the documents we had brought, until she looked up at Robert and remarked, 'Don't I know you from somewhere?'

He looked a bit dazed and toyed with the idea for such a long time that I felt the need to rescue him by proffering, 'Have you seen his photo on the inserts of CDs or tapes? He is a New Age musician.'

'No,' she said, 'but I know that face.'

I think it pertinent here to make a brief detour and tell you more about my husband.

Circa 1992, Robert and his friend Christopher Green sent a tape to a company named New World Music which was accepted. They called themselves 'Runestone' and pro-ceeded to produce a series of CDs: *Stonehenge*, *Mysteries*, *Crystal Lord* and *Swirling Dreams*. Later, when Chris branched out on his own for six years (until the two reunited under the supervision of an amazing man named Medwyn Goodall to create *Sacred Circle* and *The Lost Henge*), Robert did a solo album which he called *A State of Grace* and carried on to gain further experience with another partner he was just about to meet.

In about 1999, when I was attending a craft fair in the little village of Wadhurst, Sussex (I made wooden toys and novelties from self-devised templates, cutting the shapes out, painting and varnishing them), an extremely nice gentleman named Brian Hopper came up to me and showed an interest in the music that I had suggested Robert should display on my stall for publicity and possible sales. I asked him to stay until Robert was free because it seemed obvious to me that Brian had a great interest in music and perhaps they could try a project together. Sure enough, that transpired and they have made albums and been friends ever since. They initially composed a disc called *Virtuality*, and, more recently, another called *Just Deserts*. And so my virtual circular tour has brought me back round to Maidstone Magistrate's Court and the newly introduced Grace Morley.

'I know,' announced Grace excitedly, 'it was Rotherfield Cricket Club, did you ever play cricket for them?'

'Yes,' exclaimed Robert, 'that's where it was. Now I remember!'

That having been recognised, we all felt a great deal more at ease. Grace proceeded to explore my research documents more thoroughly, and then she gave me a couple of forms to fill in, (forms again), while she took some of my evidence away for copying, and we waited for her return. She left me in no doubt that she would do her best for me; her only hesitation was that I could not produce a letter of proof from my father or my mother to say that he was indeed my biological parent. I did have four letters which I hoped she would choose to copy from my relatively newly acquired family in Canada. They were from my brother Clive's wife Meg in Ontario, from my brother Bart in Ontario, from a cousin who worked at the National Archives of Canada at that time and finally one from Great Uncle Doyle in British Columbia, each confirming that they were convinced I belonged to their Canadian fold.

I prayed these would be sufficient, along with my

father's ID card, which had been given to me by Bart's wife, April, on their visit to us in England. It was dated 1943, clearly from when he was stationed over here in the Canadian Armed Forces. I listed additional points on the form – which, remember, I was filling in at short notice – those being that in these modern days there is a growing enthusiasm for the gathering of correct information for the drawing up of family trees and there was a strong possibility that my family generations down the line, or researchers working on their behalf, might develop an urgent need to find these facts. Therefore I felt it was not unreasonable to want my father's name listed on my birth certificate with my mother and myself, an event which undoubtedly would be a great joy and comfort to me.

If the law had provision for me to do this, Grace Morley explained, without a letter from my mother or father (both deceased), then it could be done. But I must realise that this was a very unusual case, she emphasised, although she admitted there must be others in the same situation.

The cost of swearing an oath in court is £130 as I write this particular chapter – I was prepared to pay almost anything within reason at that point. It was now in the lap of the gods.

On the way home we reminisced at how fortunate we had been in our research with all the people in the various public offices offering such willing help. We were passing a nursery school in Kent and I noticed all the teddy bears painted on the wall of the building; I couldn't believe it. Although Robert had pointed them out on the way to Maidstone I'd failed to notice them. This was so important because, when leaving our house, I had followed my instincts and picked up my brown furry bear Henry Warmheart for luck – almost a spitting image of these painted bears. I am sixty-three and in no habit of taking teddies out with me for the day, but on the way home what should we see, but all his little bear cousins. Once more my psychic ability had entertained me – not just me, US!

And that bear became my mascot for this project.

CHARMING THE BIRDS
OFF THE TREES

And when I tell them,
    (And I certainly am going to tell them),
    …
They'll never believe me,
They'll never believe me.
That from this great big world
You've chosen me!

'They Didn't Believe Me' –
written by Jerome Kern,
taken from the musical, *The Girl from Utah*

The above is an old song mother sang to me often. I asked her many a time to tell me about the person she was singing of.

'I asked him if he was married,' she said, 'and he said to me, "Really, I'm not, but hey, if you don't believe me, take a look in my wallet".' That, she said, was good enough for her, so she didn't see the need to pry.

My father, Leslie Joseph Doyle, was a Canadian soldier at the time of meeting my mother in 1939 when he was stationed in England due to the war.

He had started employment in Canada as a lumberjack; his family has provided me with the following record obtained from Might Directories Limited city directory, which proves his job movements.

1935: he became a night clerk at the Hotel Frontenac in Ontario.

1937: he became a waiter there. The entry shows that the hotel was standard, and had 'sixty rooms being modern and comfortable'.

1939: he later progressed to hotel manager, it is said, and this brings us to the period when he came to my native country and captivated my mother and where my story begins, demonstrating what our being charmed can lead to.

I feel the need once more to digress here, because I am interested in astrology. I browsed several websites, curious to see what influence the name of my birthplace, Elmwood, could have had on my entrance into our world. This diversion will also show some insight into my personality, via a colourful New Age interest that I have cultivated.

The elm tree, according to Nicholas Culpeper the famous herbalist and astrologer who lived from 1616–54, belongs to the ruler-ship of the planet Saturn which, as some people may know, is an earth sign governing knees, teeth and bones.

I am under the earth sign of Virgo (under Mercury), which is in charge of bowels and intestines – ugh, the innards – but my husband is under Saturn, interestingly enough.

The theory reads that if you know the planet that is causing your affliction, you can prescribe the plant to counteract it. Saturn is the silent reaper of time and tradition, who wears us all down eventually. He teaches us that to progress we need to have control and apply patience, thus learning to adjust to frustrations. Through this we reap the reward of becoming stronger. We put personal restrictions upon ourselves, which we can liken to the rings or boundaries placed around Saturn. This teacher of patience says to me that I did not pursue this story while my mother was alive because I exercised a moral discipline and suffering upon myself in order to save her a cruel hurt or the experience of reclaimed and unwanted memories. She was most distressed whenever I asked questions about my father at a time when I thought he may yet be found alive and subsequently suggested I find his family.

Now the time feels right for me to deal with the skeletons left in the cupboard and pursue the search. Having a healthier relationship with myself, particularly after achieving three certificates towards becoming a counsellor, the boundaries look as if they are lifting, and that claim for partial freedom from Saturn can be made. I say partial because realistically it may be too late to realise the jigsaw in entirety. I am commencing this search at the age of sixty-three. Self instruction on this subject over many years has taught me that Mercury, my ruling sign, is associated with the urge to enquire, to search and to know ourselves and the world around us, and is also connected to the art of communication. The difficulty I have is the irony of Saturn's restraining power, which we all experience to some degree. This, coupled with the influence of Mercury's characteristic of 'having to know' provokes me to cry, 'Cruel fate! Why do you give me the art of communication from the messenger of the gods, Hermes, yet cut me off by another god, Kronos, from the very sources I should have the most communication with?' That's if we believe in these things.

The first address on Mother's ID card, presumably my second home, was dated June 1943 but obviously forgotten by me at the age of one. It was in Sherborne, Dorset.

She told me that we were evacuated to Sherborne in the war, which is quite likely, but it could have been that she needed to go away with me to escape wagging tongues! How she travelled all that distance with a babe in arms, I shall never be able to imagine. We stayed there until February 1944 when the address changed – again I take this to mean it was now my third home – and we moved to 6 Beblets Cottages, Worlds End Lane, Green Street Green, Farnborough, Kent. I have explained in a previous chapter about the renumbering of this to 114 Worlds End Lane in 1971, when it came under Orpington, Kent.

Next came my fourth home, Primrose Cottage, also in Sherborne, Dorset, which I do remember. We relocated to there in March 1944, staying there until July 1946. This is a stark landmark. I was nearly four years old, so it was possible for things to happen here that would remain with me throughout my life.

I loved the animals at this place. There were at least three cats and lots of chickens; I played with them often. Auntie Fox shouted at the cats and this upset me as they were my friends. It is possible that she misunderstood me, thinking I was stupid to be concerned for the cats.

Once, Auntie Fox dragged me away from a fascinating thunderstorm I was watching from the window. I was intrigued by the lightning zigzagging down to the ground. I could have watched this for hours, having no thought of danger. However, she gave me a fear of thunderstorms until, in 1987 when the hurricane struck the United Kingdom, I could resist it no longer and found myself watching with my old passion.

There was also a son, Bernie. He was wonderful. He played with me and let me curl his hair. He showed me how to polish his army boots with spit and polish and he took me to Sherborne Castle one day where we spoke to soldiers on the walls. He made me glow.

I took so much of Bernie's time I was told, that Auntie Fox shooed me away and, when she thought I was out of earshot, she told my beloved Bernie what a nuisance I was. I hurt inside because I thought he must have had to agree with his mother. I think of him now; he was the closest I had to a father.

I don't know where my mother was most of the time. I heard she went to work and I hardly ever saw her; they left me with Effie. Oh how I wish they hadn't. Effie was Auntie Fox's own teenage daughter. Mae was her adopted teenage daughter by means of her second marriage. They said I adored Effie and even when Mum got me a pram for Christmas she told me that because Effie had to collect it for her, I always said that the pram was from Effie. I adored Effie because I had to.

One night I was tucked up in bed with a nightlight; I was afraid of the dark. Then someone crept into my bedroom and woke me as they snuffed out the light. I heard them go back downstairs, followed by giggles and stifled laughter, then groaning and wailing sounds came up the stairs at me through the air. What could a four year old do? The stairs creaked and squeaked as they, (Effie and Mae) tiptoed up and down, for effect I should imagine, but there was no aid for my absolute fear and helplessness.

I was an adult before I was able to tell the following story to my mother. Somehow I had always felt that she would be unapproachable on this topic, as she could do no better for me then. Even then, when I finally approached her with the terrible history, she could only tell me that I was a wicked, evil girl, as if I were still an ignorant and untrustworthy child.

Hands hold mine as I am led upstairs. I am alone with Effie and Mae. They take me to the big bedroom, I think at the front of the house. They tell me to get on the bed. Effie gets on top of me, and Mae watches from the foot of it. Effie wriggles around on top of me telling me how nice it is, and what a good girl I am. She keeps telling me to say it is

37

nice, isn't it, but I do not. She wants me to say that I like it, but I do not. I am puzzled, frightened and confused. There is no one to aid me. I believe I am dazed.

I am now at Walden's, St Mary Cray, Kent. (1 July 1946)

Presumably, this was my fifth home, and is also mentioned earlier in this book, where I believe there lived the three goats I so fondly remember, Adam and Eve and Pinch Me – delightful names. Mum and I watched them together after we strolled along the lane. I remember being given a rabbit's foot for comfort as I lay in my bed or cot and that is all, not surprising because, stamped on my location finder in the form of Mother's ID card, is another address for the date of 8 October 1946. Our new address and my sixth home was Goda Road, Littlehampton, Sussex. I was still only four years old. I touched on this address in the 'Amethyst Incident', but now I'd like to expand on it.

My mother's birthday is the 12 October 1917. She can't have had much of a birthday that year, poor soul. Could it be that I remember arriving there, drawn by horse and cart, with minimal luggage, maybe having come from the train station? She had a sister in Littlehampton I was to discover, not that she had time to see much of her and her family, but it was better than nothing I suppose. Mother became the housekeeper for the lady of this house, Mrs Searle.

I was afraid of Mrs Searle; she seemed a fierce, scary person to a small child, frightening me so much that I even wet my pants on occasion to my shame. I was by then a nervous and timid child; writing this helps to clarify to myself as to why. But here lived Timothy, Matilda and Eustace – oh, such dear little tortoises. I loved them to bits. Tim was a great big tortoise with a pale shell, Matilda was quite big with a darker shell, as I recollect, and Eustace was just little Eustace. We polished their shells and, when it was spring, we had to take them out of their straw-filled boxes. I

38

don't know if this was part of our duties or whether we were allowed participation just for my sake. I was enthralled that they could be put in the dark all winter, and come out alive after having had no food or water for so long. We had put them into the outside loo space, packing them away safely in the autumn for what I was assured was necessary hibernation. I can imagine my concern until it was proven true for the first time.

I remember the fat, red, ripe Victoria plums that I got from the trees and fed eagerly to the tortoises who found them delicious, and the searches for big-headed, golden dandelion flowers which were likewise munched with ardour. On several occasions I had to right little Eustace as he ventured into difficulties and got upturned. I feared he'd be dead but he soon recovered when on his feet again and I was talking to him. The grown-ups had warned me he'd die if he was left upside down for too long. I loved to come out in the morning sunshine and search for my three friends, hidden as they often were until the day warmed up, under foliage or crevices or in a hole in the earth they had dug to bury themselves in. Lettuce leaves featured greatly on their menu and I would put all the creatures in a circle and the greenery in the centre so they'd make a beeline for it. Tortoises can move faster than you'd expect when it suits them. The importing of Testudos was banned in 1984 when the EEC Council agreed to treat three species of tortoise (Spur-thighed, Hermann's and Marginated) as prohibited trade and protect them as an endangered species. I do not know which type ours were, but on viewing a website it looks like they could be members of the Mediterranean Spur-thighed tortoise, but I couldn't swear to it.

Here endeth the entries on my mother's ID card. It has been a good friend and companion through these searches.

REVISITING THE TOWN OF MY WORLD WAR II EVACUATION

On 30 July 2007 Robert and I were having a week's break at Bournemouth and decided to include an investigation into my past life at Sherborne, Dorset. We arrived around 11.15 a.m., the journey having taken about an hour and a half. We headed straight to the correct road and found the fourth dwelling place, Primrose Cottage, the apparent site of our second evacuation. It was clearly signposted outside, but had a garage attached which would not have existed when I had been there. I asked some nearby workmen if this would be the original cottage, but they were not locals, so I attracted the attention of a neighbour opposite and she kindly directed us to the offices of West Dorset District Council and Sherborne Town Council.

When we arrived, we showed them my mother's ID card to confirm that the Manor House, Newlands, which was now their offices and which was stamped on our card as our first lodgings at Sherborne, was indeed the place where mother and I had stayed. They confirmed this to be one and the same building which had been re-fronted in 1820 in a Gothic-revival style, but they could not help with information about the cottage. They directed us to the Somerset and Dorset Family History Society which we found in Cheap Street, near the conduit. By this time I was tired and needing sustenance, but Robert insisted we go in there first and a receptionist came forward, very keen to help. I would like to qualify here why I am always saying I'm tired. I was told by a doctor at my local surgery that once I had faced all these things I would have more energy, as I was always feeling drained. I am grateful for his dedication to helping me through this to a better quality of life. He was there for me at eight-thirty some mornings, when I'd woken up in a panic in the night, having had flashbacks. He saw to it that I had some prompt NHS counselling.

The helper thought it very likely that we had been evacuees, and that Newlands, as they call the Manor House now for brevity, was used as a holding place. She felt that it would have taken an especially long time to house Mother and me given the circumstances, and impressed upon me how lucky I was not to have been taken from Mother and Mother to have been put into an asylum. I showed her the ID card and any information and names I could muster. She encouraged me to email her upon my return home to Crowborough, East Sussex, so that she would have time to conduct some research and maybe discover the site of the original cottage. She thought she knew some of the young family of the former inhabitants. We were quite in a state of shock as we had not expected to get so far so quickly in the way of information.

We ate our lunch eagerly, generally finding that people were very helpful and friendly. The old-fashioned ambiance of the town quite charmed us. Refreshed, we then went to visit the castles. The newest was closed but as our intent was so earnest we ventured into the grounds finding a gardener who told us what he could whilst we promised to remove ourselves as soon as we'd looked hard at the general layout and wonderful building. This we did in no time so as to keep our end of the bargain, thank you to him.

We next went to the old castle which he'd given directions for. This was open but in ruins. We could see as much as we wanted from the borders without paying the entrance fee as our time was running out, and I felt this was the place I'd come to with my favourite person, the son of the cottage family who'd been in the army, as I've formerly mentioned. We bought two lovely books with old black and white photos of the town, which I am grateful to have: *Around Sherborne* by Nicola Darling-Finan and *Sherborne and Castleton* by Rodney Legg.

As a last attempt to make the most of our visit, we chose to view the abbey, being so near to it as we were. We hadn't long as our parking meter would run out at 3.15 p.m. and we needed to complete the return journey to Bournemouth in time to freshen up and be down for dinner at 6.30 p.m. The weather this day was most conducive to being out and about, another blessing.

What an amazing ceiling it had. Legg's book mentions that it has 'fan-vaulting and bosses of late-fifteenth-century Ham stone in the nave, the best roof in Dorset', also mentioned is a memorial plaque commemorating the 'natural event' of a great hailstorm in May 1709, which caused an extraordinary flood on the site. I cannot resist adding this last piece of information, to reinforce that freak weather is not just a characteristic of our present time. This abbey warrants another visit as does the town for sure.

We went finally to the Half Moon Hotel (c1955) in Half Moon Street for a cup of tea at around 2.40 p.m. and left Sherborne at 3.15 p.m.

It now seems that I have lived in a manor house, but not quite in the manner I would have liked. Nevertheless the idea appeals to me; Newlands was amazing inside and out. It was a thoroughly enjoyable day.

The following is a copy of the email sent 10 August 2007.

You said you would remember my visit to you on the 30 July this year.

I told you that only last year – 2006 – I had managed, by two court visits and via DNA tests after finding three half brothers in Canada in 1999 and following mother's death, to have my father's name added to my birth certificate – a very rare event!

I showed you my mother's ID card from the early 1940s and told you that we had resided at the Manor House, Newlands, in Sherborne, on 4 June 1943 until 14 February 1944. Then there is a small gap where we go to Green Street Green in Farnborough (now Orpington), Kent, near where I was born, until we return to Sherborne, Dorset, to be housed in Primrose Cottage (only house address that appeared on the card, no number) from March 1944 until we left in July 1946.

We found the cottage as explained to you on that day, but you doubted whether this was the right one.

You believed that mother and I were held there, as in a holding house at Newlands, whilst we were found a suitable placement (bearing in mind Mother's situation as an unmarried mother with a child by a foreign soldier). You also said I was lucky not to be taken from her and she put in an asylum. She had said at times when cross with me that she wished she had given me to the couple who had wanted to have me. Whether that has any bearing, I do not know.

She had said we were evacuated in the war but no other details and you seemed to believe this was the case.

I gave you names of the blood daughter at that residence, Effie Fox (Wood became her name once she was married, could have been to a man named Josh) and Mae became her stepsister when Effie's mother's first husband died and she married Mae's father. These were teenagers I seem to think at the time and looked after me a lot, while Mother said she worked at a hotel or manor. Mrs Fox, who I was told to call 'auntie' (everyone was to be called that by me, although unrelated), must have been the adult lady of the house when using her first married name.

I hope you have enough to go on regarding the cottage so we can come and stay a couple of nights and find the original spot. I loved visiting Sherborne again and strangely, remembered parts. Having moved many times, places stand out like landmarks – six places before the age of five! It is lovely how it has retained its original character, long may that last.

Thank you once again for your kind interest and assistance,

Yours sincerely,

Lesley-Madeleine

P.S. Mother kept her maiden name of Steer, so I would have been Lesley Steer, born in 1942 at Elmwood (which I cannot find), in Homestead Rd, Chelsfield, Kent.

RAISING PART OF THE SPECTRE

The fresh arousal of this painful memory seems to be my only path through to the other side of my story; it is an unavoidable part taking place between 1946–1954, harking back to Littlehampton, Sussex again. Eight years; this must have been my longest stay ever as a child, therefore quite an impressionable one in a large part of my formative stage.

This however is not my secret divulged, it only scratches the surface.

I suppose that when a person shuts off their past life and enters into another one, they hope that, like a wound, the site will heal and the scab will drop off. This is hardly ever the case. The scab does drop off in the main, but a remnant stays behind it in the form of a tiny, near-invisible scar. The old baggage having not been properly handled accompanies the bearer awkwardly ever-onward.

As expected, new friends were made by both of us. There were Johnny and Celia for me, (Mrs Searle's grand-children, when they visited) and Auntie Annie for mum.

I cannot remember much about my two new pals – only that we had a lot of fun together. I seem to remember only bad things starkly. As for Annie she was kind I heard, and was the wife of Mrs Searle's gardener Clem. Clem and Annie had two adopted daughters, Maureen and Sheila. I was left with that family sometimes. Clem kept rabbits; I liked those and adored him, but when I slept over one time, I was terribly homesick for my mother. Clem saw to it that I had my own little garden plot at Mrs Searle's and I grew the tallest of tall sunflowers.

I played in the garden for long hours with Clem, while he worked, the only thing I didn't like about him was that when he found out that I detested worms, he threw them at me. Why should he do this, I used to think, if he likes me?

When we lay in bed in the mornings, Mother would make little scratching noises on the mattress, and I'd ask in wonder where was the noise coming from. 'Oh, that's the fairies,' she would laughingly say, and I readily believed her. Thinking back I suspect this was the easiest attention she could give me before she started her long day's work. In the evening I had to put myself to bed, while Mother waited on her employer who kept her standing at her bedside for what seemed like hours with the supper tray in her hand. I would listen to the series of Dick Barton Special Agent and Snowy on the radio downstairs, one hand on the door frame ready to dash upstairs to our room and to dive underneath the covers. I was so terrified yet enthralled by that programme with its over-excitable signature tune.

One day I sat by the scabious flowers, I recall those so well, their beautiful blue steeped my mind back then with a glorious presence. I got carried away by my imaginary friend Andrew ('Drew), whom I have to mention, to the extent that I left two old wax dolls in the sun until their faces melted beyond repair. I was so upset and wouldn't have realised their value until I was much older. Without 'Drew I don't know how I would have coped in this lonely life. Two cats from next door would come into the garden in hopes of a game from me, which I duly supplied.

I remember using my teddy bear as a form of release for my frustrations by often resorting to teddy bashing. I would grab him by the legs, whilst banging his head fiercely on the floor – an act I was afterwards very sorry for as a small child. What would psychologists make of that?

*

Mother and Mrs Searle orchestrated for my own good that if I didn't move my bowels I would be subjected to having a sliver of soap inserted where I wouldn't like it, then they'd wait for my gripe pains to ensue and me to produce.

To go or not to go would be the question, because if I didn't they would repeat the procedure I was sure.

If I did manage it, the pain would be excruciating because of the build up, to put this as delicately as I can.

The stress of this, let us say, 'stubborn movement' being lodged between two worlds for a long duration, as I can only explain it, occurs to me repeatedly, as the problem did not properly resolve itself over the years. I am sure this remedy would not be permitted nowadays and only added to the phobia. My fear of Mrs Searle, as previously said, would cause me to have accidents when I was very small and we met each other during the day. I can see now that my timidity along with this harsh practice on a child could have been part of the reason why.

*

I had a great shock when Mother came home one day and all her teeth were missing. I asked where they were and she said she'd been to the dentist and he directed her to have every one of her teeth out over two operations. She told me she wanted to get it over with and did it in one, but I suspect that she couldn't spare the time for a second visit. Mother was quite poorly for some time afterwards.

I did very well in the music exam at school one time, but then Mrs Searle and mother were arguing, because Mrs Searle wanted me to take violin lessons at her sister's private school for girls, and Mother said that, she didn't want me to. I think this is partly what caused the difficulties

49

between them as I was told that Mrs Searle wanted to have a stronger influence in my life.

She supplied me with books on my birthdays which would lead to deeper reading. Beatrix Potter books, *Noddy*, Ladybird and *Winnie the Pooh* came my way. My favourites were Enid Blyton's *Famous Five* series.

It was seen to that I attended Sunday School and one day two of my school friends and one enemy wanted me to play truant with them from church. I ran home to ask Mother, as I had told them, 'I can't do that until I've asked my mum!' My naïvety was apparent. I'm not sure what she replied.

When you are alone in your heart because something feels off, your classmates sense it. I must have been ten or eleven when I was sitting one day near the front of the class at Littlehampton's Junior School waiting for the teacher to arrive. A girl whose habit it was to taunt me stole to the door facing us but to our left, to check that the teacher was not coming. This was not unusual for some of the group as they often got up to pranks and wanted to know that the coast was clear first. The girl disappeared behind me, but then came the feel of hands gripped tightly about my unsuspecting neck. The shock froze me, but my mind fought to sustain my helpless body. I could not turn round, I don't know why; I did not know who the person was that held me. Not being able to gasp for breath, the effect on me was the feel of absolute fear, cold terror in my stomach and a shaky body, being rendered powerless as I was. What added to this was the sound of giggles from the colluding class. I really believed I was going to die, was she going to kill me?

The teacher arrived and the hands released me. Normality appeared to be restored before the teacher could detect my personal tragedy. However, it was not restored for me. I never recovered trust in people after this nightmarish memory had been instilled in my tired, aching brain, trying as I did to understand why people didn't like me. It was so unbelievable that I don't think I even told my mother. I buried it along with all the other incidents. This is its first telling.

Playtimes were always lonely ordeals which I dreaded. I wandered trying to make myself and others believe I was busy. This did not ease the pain, the time dragged. If I made the odd friendship I considered myself lucky, but I was insecure regarding my ability to maintain it.

Whilst I was at my last senior school at Bromley, Kent, somehow my mother obtained fresh cakes, I think from a friend who baked. On a few occasions I took some into school to offer to the classroom bullies who happened to be prefects. This was not deviously done, but conducted in order to make my frantic existence more bearable, a survival mode if you like. I soon learned that one cannot buy genuine friendship. Once the gifts were devoured with the yearned-for accompanying smiling faces directed towards me, they quickly resorted to their taunting ways. My happiness was short-lived. How I wished life would go away. My only haven was to return to the loneliness at the end of the day where, once back at the house where we then lived, I could escape into my world of imagination.

I also belonged to the Brownie pack where I was in the Sprites' group. I obtained the honour of being able to 'fly' up to the Girl Guides through passing all the tests. Not long after that we left Littlehampton and, as I write this, I am beginning to realise the reasons why.

Each time we move on in the hope of finding a better place nowhere proves to be home for me.

The opportunity arises for me to go to Guide camp; we are all just twelve years old. I get to go. How excited I must be, I have never had a holiday. (I haven't realised that before; could this be why I don't really enjoy holidays?)

We arrive and it all seems normal at first until I realise

51

that everyone seems to be avoiding me. I'm sensitive to this, so I try to make conversation and be included to no avail. I sob and ask why nobody wants to talk with me. 'We've all decided that you were going to be put into Coventry,' one proffered.

'Why?' I asked dumbly.

'Because we know something about your father that you don't,' they taunted.

My longed-for holiday became a nightmare that would never end. Several isolated days in hostile company for a damaged child. Nowhere to turn. The Brown Owl Guide leader didn't seem to notice. I went on the walks, I ate the bees in the jam and I used the latrines, blindly and numbly. I lived through the days looking for a tomorrow that would get me home, but this slow torture was what I had to endure, loveless and hopelessly. My enemy, who vied with me for my friend's company at home, sprained her ankle one day. I bandaged it in the hope that by helping her, she would look on me more favourably, although it was my nature to do this for her anyway. As luck would *not* have it, she woke groaning in the night that it was too tight and hurt her. I speedily undid it.

Our arrival home from camp was not the joy it should have been. I fell asleep over my soup that night, to find in the morning I was seriously ill and the doctor had to be called after several days of my refusal to eat. He sternly told me and the two adults that if I did not eat he would have to take me into hospital and I'd be put on a drip. They explained what that was to me later.

Eventually the story spilled out as to what had happened at camp. For the one and only time, I heard my mother crying out on the landing. Mrs Searle loomed at the door and said. 'OK, your father is not dead as you were led to believe. He has a wife and three children in Canada. This is nothing to do with you, so let there be no more said about it'.

So the children didn't speak to me because my father is still alive and has a family? Why? What does that mean?

So much unsaid, but then we left…

Much later, Mother related to me in a sad voice about a time when she was standing in a shop and very pregnant with me. She had overheard the owners who knew my father saying things about him, and that they included in the conversation the fact that he was married. She also said that she nearly fell through the floor and didn't know how she got out of the shop.

My last memory of Mrs Searle was as I climbed the stairs, met her as she stood facing me at the top and was instructed to say goodbye. She turned away after kissing me and, cupping my face in her hands, she was so distraught that she nearly pushed me down the stairs. Now, did we go because she did not like the reasons she had maybe freshly learned as to why I had been scorned? Or, was it that my mother needed to remove me from those spiteful children? Once more I find a situation where the connecting riddle will never reveal its answer for me.

This move from Littlehampton in my pre-teens had followed my mother's wake-up call which, in my discernment, alerted her to the fact that I may be near to discovering a 'skeleton in the cupboard'. She successfully guarded this until her death in 1996 and I did not find out until 1999. I term this 'my secret' although she appeared to have deemed it to be hers alone.

THE EDMUNDS AND WALDENS

A surprise was in store for me. I had emailed Jenny, the person whose family I had resided with at St Mary Cray, Orpington, Kent after the hasty retreat from Littlehampton. It appears that I had previously lived with this family when I was two years old but I had not been told.

The family consisted of Mr T and Mrs J Edmund, and their three children: Ted, Victoria and Jenny (in age order).

Tim was not my uncle but I called him that and I called Janice 'Auntie Janice'. He teased me relentlessly I believe, and I did not know what to make of him. Nevertheless we were under his roof and I was to be good and cause no trouble as usual. I remember preparing mountains of potatoes for the family mealtimes and I resented it. I played with Jenny but do not remember anything significant about Victoria or her older brother Ted. Auntie Janice, their mother, did not leave a great impression on me either, but Jenny, that was another story, Jenny certainly did.

Now that I can look through a rear view mirror I know that these different people have all caused me to react in various ways. I broke Victoria's nose because she tickled my ribs and I jerked up suddenly, but I can drop the guilt because I now know that it was a normal reaction for someone who couldn't bear to be tickled.

I badly bruised Auntie Janice's face whilst on a caravan holiday with them. The wind was howling outside and Janice had gone out for something. She came back pleading for someone to quickly open the door as it was also raining. My instinct told me no, but Jenny and Victoria, who were both inside with me, insisted with urgency that I do as I was told. I opened the door, the vicious wind fatefully drove it forcefully into her face and she was marked for weeks. I felt awfully ashamed and I was being blamed by the Edmunds for both incidents. I cannot prove it, but that is how it felt and still feels.

I played with Jenny and found her to be a most unusual person, she was both daring and bold. To speak to her now she is extremely intelligent and amusing. Her armoury of words appeals to me enormously.

They had a lovely golden retriever dog named Sandy and I adored him. He was gentle and docile. I now know that he was bought as a pet for Ted, but I was led to believe originally that he was a war dog running between lines in the army and working with Tim. It appears this may have been Tim's sense of humour. When Sandy died we all mourned him relentlessly.

I remember once being out with Jenny when she dug up some old, corroded false teeth and to my absolute horror she put them in her mouth and scared me to death. She laughed as she always would, but I believe it was shortly after this that she developed meningitis. I swear now that her feat of devilry was the cause of her illness, she was in a serious way. Luckily and thankfully she made a full recovery.

We lived in an area which had a common in the middle of a half-moon of houses and the gypsies would habitually tie up their horses there, so every day I could take pleasure by looking over or walking out to see these lovely creatures. Jenny's family always had chickens and I recall times when they kept white mice; there were always cats around too. Once my mother had gone to work on a Sunday at Farnborough Hospital, Kent, where she was the deputy matron's personal maid and I was so yearning for her. Jenny had two new kittens and wouldn't let me hold even one. I cried and was heartbroken. I think Auntie Janice must have said then that she should let me hold one, and I did, but I was so unhappy there without my mum.

Jenny taught me about people being hard.

Uncle Tim died in the late 1990s (as far as I remember) and at his funeral Jenny confessed to me that she had always disliked me because I was held up to her by her parents as the model of perfection. I hadn't known this, but told her I understood. I realised that Jenny may well have thought this as I was always told by my mother that I should be seen and not heard and so I never used to cause any fuss.

She must have thought me mature enough to handle the truth, but, 'Hey, Jenny, it was your dad's funeral. He had given me away at my wedding, and I am a sensitive person, ow!' Her intelligence hadn't served her well there or she would have realised that some juvenile cuckoo in another's nest has to be discreet or get kicked out if spotted causing any grief to the rest of the chicks!

For example, Mum used to say that I must certainly not cry on my birthday. If I did, she would then say it meant I would cry the whole year through. She made absolutely certain that I knew never to touch or use any of other people's possessions in their households. I assume this was because people's belongings were precious to them and she didn't want me to spoil or break anything. In other words, it soon became clear that under no circumstances would these homes ever be my own and we were always silently in fear of being moved on, whether it was true or not. Therefore, it must have seemed as though I was always being perfect when I was left with the families for long hours, but never created any commotion which could have put us in a bad light.

Jenny tells me that her father (Mr Tim Edmund) had

joined the Welsh Guards in 1932 and was recalled in 1939. He served in Gibraltar, France, North Africa and Italy. He was awarded the Military Medal as well as relevant campaign stars and a War Medal. He was mentioned in dispatches for going out repeatedly under enemy fire to repair telegraph wires. Jenny states he was assigned to guard the Russians and Poles who were being held and then sent back to certain death at Stalin's hands. All part of the deal brokered by Stalin, Roosevelt and Churchill if I've understood it correctly.

He did not want to talk about it and everyone can respect him for that.

Now we come to the part where I received Jenny's reply in April 2006 giving me Victoria's current phone number among other bits of information that I had requested. I plucked up the right mood to contact Vicky, never knowing what I might encounter.

When I spoke to her she sounded very bright and encouragingly friendly and it was nice to contact her again. She proceeded to enlighten me in any way she could.

Apparently the Edmund family, (minus Jenny who had not yet been born), all lived at Walden's (on Mother's ID card) where Tim had been a warden for an insurance company.

On this spot had originally stood a big house called Orpington House where some people called the Taylors or Tailors lived and bred Orpington chickens. There was a walled garden with orchards. They were wealthy and the poultry houses were in the fields.

They built a house next door which they called Walden's.

The Parrots, who are on my baptism card as sponsors for me, bought Walden's with, I believe, the Edmunds already in residence. One day they turned up with my mother and me in tow and we moved in together with them, so my memory of them there proved true! Mother then became the housekeeper. This is how I understood it from Vicky. She tells me that it was a typical house where the servants had their own quarters, reached via the back stairs. The owner occupants of course used the main staircase. I asked if Mother and I were in the same rooms as them and she said, 'No,' and that we had our own room together. I would have been two years old.

I remember clearly that there had been three goats – Adam, Eve and Pinch Me – because Mother and I talked about them for years afterwards, but Vicky cannot remember them.

The Taylors returned at the end of the war and turned the Edmunds out immediately according to Vicky, and shortly afterwards, my mother and I followed. Had they allowed her extra time as she had a small child? Maybe they just wanted their house back. Or could it be that it was because they found it had harboured a then-frowned-upon mother and baby, we shall never know. But when they left, Vicky said, there were bombing trails all the way to Biggin Hill Air Field, Kent.

So now I have it that I had already lived in the same accommodation as the Edmunds before I arrived at their privately owned house in St Mary Cray at the age of twelve. I started a second secondary school there. I have a stark remembrance of having to cut up a bull's eye in science and feeling terribly sick, and not being excused this dreadful act of sacrilege done by one who adored animals of any type.

I do wish these supposedly 'humane' humans realised the impact these lessons have on the young. Maybe they do know and don't care. I left there in time to start yet a third secondary school called Aylesbury School for Girls, Bromley, Kent, some time before the age of fifteen. My mother compelled me to leave school and find work once I reached fifteen years old, against all advice given her to the contrary by my headmistress she told me subsequently.

It might be interesting to note as I write this in August 2007 that Jenny moved after her mother's death to Worcestershire. Sadly we received the following email in Summer 2007 describing the effect of the serious flooding experienced by thousands in that area of the country.

When asked how she had fared in the floods she answered this:

Well, yes and no… Yes, in that the cats and I are all safe, if a little damp. No, because the bungalow was flooded, front to back. The rain caught me by surprise: I was in Evesham, doing my little job and then visiting an elderly friend, and then found I just couldn't get back to Moor – believe me, I had some hairy moments, ploughing through flood water and praying the car wouldn't stall out or worse. I tried every which way to get back home, and at 6 p.m. had to give up and go to a friend's house and stay there. I phoned my next-door neighbour, and she checked on the cats and made sure they were as OK as they could be, but then told me my house had water right through it. Well, save the awful details for another time, but I finally managed to get back here on Saturday after hitching a lift on a lorry when they were able to plough through the flood water on the road. Even then, I had to wade through the whole village, nearly up to my knees at times, and let me tell you – no one lets you know how bloody cold flood water is!

The bungalow had about an inch of water through it, but my neighbour Liz had been mopping out all morning by the time I got home. Other bungalows in the close were less flooded than mine because people were here to put down towels and anything else they had, but of course I wasn't here. I have learned that French windows leak – badly. The back garden remained under water for two more days, only gradually subsiding to the quagmire it now is. My entire veggie crop will have to be junked. In the house, the carpet and vinyl were soaked, and my wonderful neighbours came round and helped me rip the lot up and take it outside, then swab the whole place down with Dettol. The insurance company have been notified and will attend when they can, but Chem Dry are coming to bug-and-heaven-knows-what-else-spray the whole place on Saturday. They can only say 'some time between 7 a.m. and 10 p.m.' but they will be there. Yikes! So, I am just about to try and find an unflooded cattery to get the cats in, otherwise it will be four hours in cat cages in the car!

It's not been a nice experience with one notable exception: I think I must have the nicest neighbours in the whole world, really. They were working through the night to keep the water out of their own house (only partially successfully) but they still found time to attend to my cats, and then help me with the bulk of clearing out, swabbing down, etc. Alan came round with his Henry machine and vacced as much moisture as he could from the screed and the carpet trapped inside my fitted units.

Right now I am trying to clear things away to let air into the house, mostly to stop the smell (don't even ask!) and spraying everywhere with Zoflora. The garage is still wet through, but drying very slowly. We plod on. Thanks for thinking about me. Will catch up with rest of news in due course, but forgive me if that takes a little longer than usual.

Hope all is well with you.

Love,

Jenny

APPREHENSION

It was with much apprehension that I fumbled with the envelope that arrived this morning, 24 March 2006. I had been torn between opening it then, or waiting until later. I had fed myself positive thoughts for the whole of the time since applying to the court and receiving an answer as to whether I could make a declaration of parentage to have my father put onto my newly acquired full certificate with Mother and me. The postman came down our drive as we were in our red Mini Cooper about to go out; he handed the letter through the car window at my request.

Opening this and facing a 'no' would be an end to it.

I prevented myself from welling up with emotion as I read the contents of the letter, which in no way blocked my path, nor gave me permission for a father's entry onto the document, but did imply that I should construct a case for myself and at an appropriate time organise a court date with them for my appearance. This was great news and the fee involved did not act as a deterrent as the meaning of this invitation for me was far more important than the outlay of money or effort.

The only witness available to call was eighty-six-year-old Cathleen Adams. She was my mother's old friend from before the war days (1936) until Mother's death in 1996.

I feel it would be unreasonable to drag the elderly lady to the court, bearing in mind how draining the journey from Northampton, where she lives now, can be. Adding to this, there is a possible stress factor to consider from the impact of having to recall old memories and lost friends. I also knew that she had recently had a leg operation and had not fully recovered. Therefore I decided to leave it to 'the powers that be', as I believe that providence has always lent a hand to me.

However, her restrictions did not preclude me from writing a short statement for Cathleen to sign and date, saying that she knew my mother, and she had no reason to doubt that Mr Doyle was my father. I rang her immediately upon realising what I would need from her and disclosed my request. She did not hesitate and exclaimed that she would be happy to do this for me and if that wasn't sufficient she would even appear for me in court, her son Darren would bring her. I told her that I was exceedingly grateful and that her statement would probably be what would clinch the case if it had a chance of being successful. I ran off to post the framework of the affidavit (which my solicitor had supplied) to her whilst the idea was hot off the press so to speak. I remembered that Auntie Cath, as I had to address her from childhood, had been a rotund and jolly, hospitable lady, she sounded as sharp as a button on the phone which indicated to me that nothing had changed and her reliability need not be called into question.

Whilst I am referring to her I see this as an appropriate time to recall my eighth place of residence with Mother, a one-roomed flat with shared bathroom in Bromley, Kent. I was often left with Cathleen who had always lived at Bromley, while my mother worked at Farnborough Hospital, Kent.

Cath would take me to work with her sometimes as it was not possible for me to go with my mother. Darren was eleven years younger than me, and it fell to me to keep him amused or play with him which I now realise was generally expected of me at most of the places I was left at where there were children, but I was happy to fulfil the role here. Auntie Cath appeared to be more like what I would expect of a real aunt. She treated me in a loving way and as one of the family, although she was only my mother's dear friend. She called me 'Her Les', as she always had, only the other day, and she would address me as 'love'. Alas, neither of these endearments were used by my mother in regard to me, yet the latter she reserved for Cathleen constantly.

Cathleen's husband, Bill, was also quite kind to me and taught me how to play chess. He made stuffed toys for the children in Great Ormond Street Hospital in London. He was formerly a tailor so this came naturally to him.

They liked cats and one was called 'Miss Tiggy Anderson'. This so appealed to my sense of humour, although Mother said I was like my father and didn't have one! I've since worked on that. To reiterate, Bromley was the third secondary school that I attended. I was put straight into the A-stream because of my ability for English; never for maths.

We shared the upstairs of the two-storey house with an old lady, Mrs Collins, who would drink Guinness at night and pace the landing cat-a-wailing like a mad woman. We had two rooms at first and she had one.

When her shenanigans later grew worse, Mother and I would curl up together on a mattress we had dragged into the front multi-purpose room (lounge, diner, kitchen, without running water or sink) from the bedroom, as this door, unlike the other, had a working lock and key. We would lie there shaking and cringing with fear.

I went to the council offices in desperation one day after school, taking on this responsibility although only in my early teens. I reported, among other things, my mother's distressed state, the way we had been forced to live in fear and having sleepless nights locked in our room on the floor. I reported it because my mother was afraid to. She probably nervous that she would jeopardise our secured accommodation, but I knew that something had to be done.

Unannounced, the council arrived later that day to find our mattress on the front room floor, confirming my story. Mrs Collins was assessed and shortly after taken away to a home. The thought had never entered my head that she might be taken, not merely reprimanded for her behaviour and that this would mean that the landlady next door could let us expand to the rest of the upper floor if it suited her, rather than renting it out to somebody else. In hindsight I wonder how the landlady would have felt when found to be letting a single mother and teenage child share two rooms next to a demented old lady, and the pair of them having no hot water or sink (we washed up in a bowl filled from the shared bathroom or boiled in the kettle) and just one coal fire in the front room for heating, unless we lit the cooking stove. We went down the stairs and out the front door, then around the front of the house and through the back gate to the back garden to get fuel from the air-raid shelter at the end of the garden. Even I am breathless after saying all this. Imagine retracing our steps with a heavy load, after struggling about often in harsh weather trying to complete the task as hastily as possible.

How grateful my mother must have been to me or our landlady, I will never know as she didn't say. Having lived here without hot water and partial use of the bathroom (we had taken a bath from the kind lady, Mrs Donnelly, downstairs once a week) until the old lady was carted away.

Now it transpired we could at last have full use of the bathroom upstairs, not just the sink and loo. We could return to our usual bedroom and the old lady's room became our kitchen with sink and dining table (awaiting the hot water connection which followed shortly afterwards) but still no central heating I regret. The front room was now our lounge. Life was hard, but it had become easier.

When I came in from senior school in the winter

months, I had to light the gas stove to warm my poor cold hands and regain use of them. I had always suffered greatly from the cold. When having to walk to infant school in bitter weather at Littlehampton, there was one time when a teacher had to thaw me out and ring my mother to come and get me.

However, to return to the Bromley story. Once I had use of my hands I would peel the vegetables for dinner. They were long days for me as they started with a paper round beforehand, at Mother's insistence I'm sure.

Some neighbours would often give us plants for the garden after seeing me weeding it so enthusiastically for Mother in the more clement weather, I believe they thought I had deserved them.

I had to pay for my own clothes and a bike on the never-never. If I didn't have the money Mum would pay for it upfront on condition that I paid back a certain amount weekly. An agreement cast in stone (no leniency could be shown that I would afford my boys later on). I do believe that she just couldn't manage to keep me.

When I was fifteen and ready to leave school, Mother told me that the school had wanted me to go on to a technical school. Despite this, she said I must go out to work, even though they had offered to pay for my uniform.

This reminded me of the time when I should have taken the eleven-plus while at Mrs Searle's but Mother wrote a letter to say I was too nervous and had me excused. I have to say that at that time I was relieved, but looking through the rear view mirror again, I see it may have been a disservice.

Une enfant unique? Yes. Spoilt? No.

I was to stay at this flat until I married my first husband, Hugo, who I met at the age of fifteen. He being one year older than me, we courted for five long years before we tied the knot. To this day I still never know if he just felt compelled after a long engagement, or plain sorry for me.

His family had a big house in my book, although really just a normal dwelling by everybody else's touchstone. What he thought of our humble abode only he could tell you, if he cared to remember. I was desperately seeking love and maybe a comfort figure. But hey, all this is another chapter.

At fifteen when I left school I went to work at Marks and Spencer Ltd, claiming to Mother that I would have to practise maths at their expense. I was a sales assistant. My mother wrote to them after a while when I had commented that a friend of mine had been made a supervisor. I felt so embarrassed when they called me to the office and questioned me about my disappointment at not being offered that position. I can reflect now that my mother had obviously not considered that I lacked the confidence required for this.

In order to progress from a sales girl I went up to London, New Bond Street on my own without telling anyone and applied to be a showroom model with the Lucy Clayton Modelling Agency, which was the only other likely job I thought I might be able to succeed in. I remember a scene with Hugo when I returned from the day trip. I didn't understand why he was so furious that I would want to follow this vocation, but I later detected that he harboured the fear that it wouldn't be respectable. I was hurt that he didn't know that this would never be an option for me.

I have the letter from the modelling agency saying that it was most unusual but as I showed talent they would be paying for my training in advance. I had no money and would be expected to pay it back as I got work and received wages. I gained a grade B in the catwalk examinations, which I was told was a high and rare achievement at that time.

I have a vivid memory of one of my visits to the agency in London and seeing Una Stubbs there. She starred with Alf Garnet and Cherie Blair's father, Tony Booth, in the popular TV comedy programme, *Till Death Do Us Part*. I presumed she may have been waiting for modelling work, or meeting a friend.

I went to a party in London one evening with Hugo who, being in the advertising business, had some useful and interesting contacts. Nerys Hughes from the TV series *The Liver Birds* was present. She was so quiet I could hardly believe it was her.

Early on, I declined a job which involved showing off corsetry and bras which could have made me a lot of money. Hugo said he was scared that he and everyone else would see my half-clad body when he travelled up and down the escalators in London's underground. I agreed with him. I had been approached about this at the photo fair in London.

Once, I applied for permission from the manageress of Marks & Spencer to have the day off in order to go to the Waldorf Hotel in London for a modelling competition. She flatly refused.

I took the risk anyway, went to London and entered the contest regardless. I came second out of many girls. The top four being chosen to model at the Photo Fair, Olympia. I was eighteen at the time. Unfortunately for me, she had seen me the previous night on TV and charged at me the next morning on the shop floor with anger spitting forth like fire from her lungs. *Oh god*, I thought, *now I've done it*, but a most unexpected thing occurred. The head manager, whose name was Mr Mulligan and whom I did my best to avoid owing only to painful timidity, came bounding to my rescue putting himself between me and her. 'No,' he said. 'Leave her alone.' In front of everyone she was prevented from expending her furious self on me. If I had liked her I would have felt pity at that instance. Later I was approached by the office staff who asked for my account of the event and a photo, from any taken, suitable to be shown in the Marks & Spencer store magazine, how glowingly wonderful I felt inside.

Later I joined H Price & Sons in a New Bond Street showroom working for Mr Price as a model. I was fond of him, but he frightened me as all men did. I expect it was because I was unused to them owing to their absence in my upbringing.

I had many frustrations at this age, always having to bottle up my anger. It wouldn't do for the person in the flat below to hear us arguing, nor the landlady living beside us, and my mother seemed to provoke me by often saying I was bad like my father, but not telling me why. She taunted me with the idea that my friends, and I had precious few at any time, would not like me if they knew what I really was like. How do you think that made me feel? No one, nowhere to turn to. Poor stressed out Mum, do you wonder at the fact that I threw milk up the wall once in sheer desperation when I could no longer contain my hurt? Neither could she, no doubt. Later in life I wrote letters to my father and mother separately, as part of my therapy, one of which is included at the end of this chapter.

Looking back at the above chapter, I realise what a brave, courageous but fiery person I have been, but usually I note, after being driven. My shameful anger is also the instigator of my courage. I am trying to manage my aggression now, but in hindsight if I lose this, do I lose my bravery? Perhaps not, if it is satisfactorily re-channelled.

Auntie Cath's affidavit arrived on 28 March 2006. Dear Cath, how grateful I am to her. She had returned the signed and dated statement immediately with additional infor- mation. This item could be the critical factor in my court case. It explained how long she had known my mother, and stated that she had no reason to believe that Leslie Joseph Doyle was not my father.

At about the same time as Cathleen's completed affidavit arrived I received a letter from Her Majesty's Court service, giving me permission to be heard in court.

28 August 1999

Dear Mum,

I am looking at a photo of me as a child and also as I am now.

It is clear that although the same little girl is in me, she is also grown up and should be allowed to have thoughts of her own, not those of other people's that are programmed in me for their own purposes.

I don't condone what you did to me (as above mentioned) but I do understand it now. I have decided that I can't hate you, and I want to defend you as you are not here to defend yourself. Because that belief is also part of my system (we should not speak ill of the dead).

I know what it is like to try your hardest against unbeatable odds and the frustrations and exasperations at being at one's wit's end to be a good parent alone. To keep coming up against yourself when this tiredness hits and your patience snaps. We try to be perfect but have to reluctantly admit that we are not.

So I'm glad that on reflection I don't hate you and I think you must have loved me in your own way.

(I have trouble with people trying to order my life but now I think that if they can't have any say at all then they might as well not be there. Where does one draw the line?)

Love,

Lesley

HERE BE DRAGONS!

My appealing letter to the court before my appearance:

April 2006

I am addressing this issue because ignoring it has not worked well for me in the past. You can see by my mother's ID card that I had six homes by the age of four, counting where I was born in Homestead Road, Green Street Green in 1942. This pattern of unrest and never having anything concrete to hold onto or any role model to copy never ceased throughout my life. Mother wasn't with me, she had to work. I was left with anyone who would have me at any given time; inevitably I was abused. She came from an orphanage in Guernsey to Britain at the age of twelve and was later put into service, so I had no family on her side. I only tell you this because it is important for you to see how much I need something from all the nothings.

People living in the twenty-first century have a one world dream but surely before I can join in that revelation my priority should be to realise a one whole person birth registration and I will give you any proof I can.

I am half Canadian, which is important to me and how I feel about myself. I have been denied the right to claim this part of me as will any future generations following on from me in a modern world of family trees.

My mother told me my father's name from the start. I want them on my certificate together as would be normal.

I have been denied being able to put him on my two marriage certificates of 1962 and 1979 as I understood it from her. I have carried my mother's maiden name through life until I was twenty. I have not had the implied peripheral trimmings of two-sided families. Can I not have this one thing which, alas, would still leave my past life wanting?

Lastly and most important, I wish to draw attention to the letter I wrote to the National Canadian Archives in 1994 which clearly indicates that I knew my father's army number and position as hotel manager at the stated hotel among other things for as long as I can remember, and before finding my three brothers in 1999.

I wish to obtain this for myself and others like me. I believe it is not illegal to put unmarried parents' names together on documents of their offspring's birth now as it was in the war years.

Thank you for taking the time for this.

Lesley-Madeleine

I made my court appearance yesterday, which was Victoria Day in Canada, in the Tunbridge Wells County Court, Kent. The appointment was for 2.45 p.m. and the judge's name was Judge Polden. He was not in robes, I saw him in his chambers, so it was very informal although he did videotape the interview.

From time to time he turned off the machine while we exchanged side issues, such as him commenting on what a fascinating and historical case it was, away from his usual territory, and remarking on how much work I had put in and the timeline through which it expanded.

He had already read my extensive file of which I possessed an identical one with the original documents in for us to peruse together. He didn't seem too interested at this point in the affidavit that Cathleen had exerted her energy on regarding her long-standing relationship with Mother, sacrificing her double bed for my parents to bill and coo in (as Father was in barracks and Mother was working in service at that time) and having to sleep on the couch as her husband Bill was away at sea. He overlooked the fact that her son Darren had transported her to the solicitors to swear on oath, or that Cath knew without doubt that Les Doyle was my father.

Judge Polden chuckled about the bed incident, but didn't mention my brother's letter of being confident that I was his sister. Instead, he decided that the four of us half-siblings, that is, three brothers in Canada (whom I had visited twice) and I in the UK should take a DNA test. I posed the question that my Canadian sister-in-law April (Bart's wife) had raised, thinking that the tests would be too watered down to be able to tell anything, but he quashed that by saying that things were much improved nowadays and he was sure that a half-sibling test would give the required knowledge we sought for a happy conclusion.

While I sat there he phoned the testing company, Cell-mark, and inquired to this fact and they confirmed he was correct in his thinking, he then asked for a quote for me and they informed us that it would be £620 plus VAT plus small samples, whatever they were. He reminded me to assure the brothers that no blood work was involved and the test was entirely voluntary.

We chatted for a while about my age and other details and he asked if I knew my brothers' full names and birth dates. I then gave my answer in the positive for having the tests conducted, because I knew that this would be too big a thing to accomplish without the court's help and direction and we are all getting older, said with a smile on my face.

Here are the Doyle brother's details given in descending order:

Bart, born 1936

Jake, born 1937

Clive, born 1939

He then confirmed my age with me:

Lesley-Madeleine, born 1942

The judge then wrote out the order for DNA testing which he reiterated would not be blood driven, only quick and painless mouth swabs; apparently many people have phobias about needles. This would be sent to me in a couple of days' time with the deadline he had set of six weeks, i.e. 3 July for me to return the report to him. After that he told me, the court would set another date for me to return and hopefully they would be able to give me the answer and action I sought.

Our passing shot, as I left with the DNA company's printed-out details, was that we hoped to goodness the results were conclusive, because I would be in a worse mess if all the history I had owned were proven null and void in one fell swoop. I told him with a laugh that it did not bear thinking about!

But dragons definitely could be lurking here which I will have to cull if this be the case and I have *no* known father! Then I shall be as a child wandering alone in the desert. I could then ask myself, has my bravado taken a turn to foolishness?

I returned home via a tea shop with my husband and binged on a huge forbidden piece of chocolate cake with him, we mulled things over, and I entered the house of one mind, being that the five following phone calls must be made that night. Firstly to Cathleen, who'd sworn the affidavit, to catch her up on progress. Also to Bart, whose wife Alice answered and agreed to the testing for him. She volunteered to email his doctor's details to me, for the samples to be sent there, as soon as he had found a doctor. His had disappeared off the face of the earth. No reflection on him I hope. Then to Clive, who answered yes immediately also, and got me his details after a short wait, although it seemed long; and finally to Jake, whose grandson told me to call back in an hour as he was out walking, which I did. This time Jake's wife Julia answered and we had a chat. She told me she had pneumonia and she sounded poorly. She said she had heard news of my recent scare of suspected appendicitis from Bart, and then answered 'yes' for Jake although she was prepared to get him. I was to ring back later that night when the details should be waiting.

One thought that did occur to me was that Monday was the only day that Cellmark were open to phone calls up to 7 p.m. The rest of the week they close their lines at 5.30 p.m. How lucky was I? I would not have had time to phone Cellmark after finding out how many kits to order on any other evening had I returned from court at this same time. That seemed spooky to me.

By the 22nd however, I only had Clive's doctor's details.

I spoke to Karen at Cellmark; she said if I contact them I must use my case number each time, they would allocate me one and add a covering note onto the form I fill in for them to highlight the court's deadline of six weeks.

On 23 May, via a phone call back to Jake in Canada, I got his doctor's details. I awaited Bart's doctor's details which arrived by phone on 25 May.

Alice told me that it was nearly impossible to register with a doctor in their town as the waiting lists were spilling over. Her doctor had agreed to do the test, but apart from that Bart hadn't got one!

Shock and horror. I phoned my doctor's surgery to arrange my swab test, fully expectant of them being compliant, and they said they didn't do it, because their practice manager had surmised that their budget didn't allow for it on the National Health Service schemes perimeter set up. I interrupted to say that we knew we had to pay and were willing. They then said that they still couldn't do it as it might be seen as trying to coerce payment from me.

'What, even if we had approached and asked you off our own back?' I blurted out.

'No, we cannot,' they said. 'It might not be construed that way, we can't risk it.'

On a repeat call, made by my husband this time, to question it, they confirmed what they had conveyed to me as true, but did give the name of another practice in the town of Crowborough, called Saxonbury House, which might have been able to do the test for me.

I duly rang and they said they would look into the details and hopefully would ring back shortly. What a nightmare. However, all looked as if it would go well with them – Saxonbury House – although I had been kept on the phone for ages with the usual music and apologies playing which one tends to get nowadays.

Robert and I went off to court to collect the order for the four tests. I then had to arrange an extension of the deadline for the tests to be back to court, changed from 3 to 17 July as we looked like running over the time window. The clerk said the judge had to write an order for it, but I said that Judge Polden had told me that I could just ring to enable this if things looked like getting tight. Thus it was agreed that they would grant it to me, I had to check when I should collect that.

Once we had confirmation of the agreed extension we treated ourselves to a break from all this by going to see *The Da Vinci Code*, which didn't wind my beliefs up as I had suspected it might. We thought it very well done. We had scampi and chips nearby afterwards and came home to find a message that the Saxonbury doctor's practice could not do my test either!

I was starting to despair and had to divert to my fall-back plan, which was a discarded Samplers List originally supplied by Cellmark with their DNA testing information brochure, which I had felt that I wouldn't need.

I found the Dunorlan Practise in Tonbridge, Kent, who agreed to conduct the test as long as I made sure they had the kit before arriving for my appointment as they have had many missed ones and this would also confirm that I was going to turn up.

Now it seemed that we were all covered by a doctor and mine was prepared to carry out the procedure on 6 June 2006.

Three of us dutifully attended our appointments but Jake kept dragging his feet to the extent that I detected he was unhappy with it. Therefore in fairness I took him off the list even though I thought I would lose my money as he had already agreed that the kit be sent to his doctor's practice and it had already been posted; I knew this for a fact because Cellmark keeps its clients up to date on progress. I had paid, as required, upfront. Fortunately for me the company offered to refund the money for his test once I explained the situation. We heard from Bart that Jake's doctor did a runner shortly after this.

Cellmark were quick, efficient and helpful and I cannot fault them. It is a most convenient way of getting a family scattered about the globe tested en bloc.

Actually I had not needed the court extension as the remaining results arrived in time for the first allotted date which the court had set, thus enabling a smooth passage. I would not hesitate to use them again.

WITH TONGUE IN CHEEK!

It is with a certain smile that I have to admit the possibility here that my father will be proved after all not to be my father.

The DNA testing was in progress and having reached my appointment day (Tuesday 6 June 2006 – ominously 666) some thoughts not entertained before were now entering my head:

a)   If this was not my father, then who was? There was one other man at that time that Mother said showed a liking for her.

b)   That would mean that my mother was not the faithful thing to him that she always swore she was.

c)   That might mean she said to herself upon my presenting myself to her in her womb with the first symptoms of pregnancy, 'Now what shall I say to this child regarding her father? I have this photo, he is dead, killed in the war... You must forget him? Easy. Yes.'

d)   On rooting out photos of Mother from when I was a fresh and unsuspecting fifteen year old, I do notice that she tended to stand beside the man in a group in preference to women, usually they were thin on the ground so this was difficult to do and she did have an engaging smile toward them and an encouraging look, and yet I've never known her have an affair with any men. Could this discomfort on my part, witnessing these frozen images, reflect what I fear may have happened in the war years? That would not have been so unnatural after all.

Now I am addressing this all these fears are confronting me.

Tuesday 6 June 2006

The DNA swab was completely painless, not a lot to ask in order to ensure that the man we took as my father, indeed was.

I arrived at 8 a.m., on time. Dr Palmer on the other hand was five minutes late – his prerogative I suppose. He was charming and shook my hand as I entered the room, making me feel special. I had already paid the charges at reception.

We went through the forms together, whereupon he asked me to spell my names, check my birthdate and state which of the ancestry options applied to me.

'I'm British,' I said.

'No,' said he, 'not that, it's not an option.' I was flummoxed.

So he kindly went through the line of Father's family, starting in Ireland, then settling for many generations in Canada, and finally ending with me being born in England.

Then together we traced mother's ancestry again coming from Ireland to the Channel Islands and then to here in the United Kingdom.

'I am not allowed to tell you what to put,' said Dr Palmer, 'but it appears Caucasian to me.'

'Well you only have to look at me to see I am white skinned,' I laughed.

So once agreed on this, we both signed the form and

signed the two required photos, which he then stapled firmly to the form. He departed from the room for a moment to fetch a rubber stamp to endorse it with.

He next took a very long, orange stick with a blue spongy bit on the end and wiped it several times on both sides of my inner cheeks, upper and lower. Dr Palmer offered that for a short while up to a paper tab which had come in a sealed package, a large, pink, round, palette-shaped dot absorbed my ID product, the satisfactorily completed exercise could be determined he told me when I asked, by the fact that the pink turned white.

The envelope with its precious contents had a tab to seal it and then went inside a plastic container, and then another which was its posting envelope. 'It's tamper-proof when sealed,' stated Dr Palmer.

I asked if it would be posted back to Cellmark that same day and he affirmed it.

He did say that I must have had reasons of my own for doing this test as he doesn't do that many of them and those are usually young children or enquiring young people curious about their paternity.

He had said that he had happily turned out to see me an hour before he would normally start his working day, so I thought at least I could answer his inquisitiveness with my reasons for being there. He seemed very interested and shook my hand again on our parting, adding his good wishes.

There I thought, not too difficult after all. I had been impressed by his professional service, and the worst part was the traffic in and out of Tonbridge!

Now for the wait, now for the results, how exhilarating is that?

FINDING THE BROTHERS

This story was not intended to be solely about the finding of my brothers, but about my persistence in having my father's name added to my birth certificate and the secret that my mother had kept locked up in her heart away from me, from my birth to her grave.

In 1998 our computer broke down again and upon its return from being mended I sat down almost in a trance as though something had possessed me. I was going to find my brothers at long last I was sure but didn't know how.

My husband came and joined me and he found the online version of the Canadian phone directory. There were 500 Doyles (rather like our Smiths) but only forty-nine Bart Doyles. Neither Jake nor Clive were listed, and I was only sure of Bart's, the eldest brother's name. I determined that I would ring five a night until I'd tried them all. This was New Year's Eve at 10 p.m. our time, (they are five hours behind us). The correct Bart Doyle was the fifth!

I was fifty-six at the time and couldn't believe after all these years that I was hearing the voice of my brother's wife who answered. I had asked her if he was the Bart Doyle, son of Leslie Doyle, who had other brothers, possibly two. She confirmed this, and I said I think you may be talking to his sister, I'm ringing from England! She did not seem too taken aback by that and said she'd go and get him. He did seem slow at responding and lost for words as I repeated to him that I was phoning from England.

His wife told me her name was Alice as she took the phone back off him, and asked me to give him a little while to digest this information, which in fact they were not surprised to hear. He told me in a later conversation that his first instinct was to hop on a plane and come straight to England, but then realised that the rest of my brothers were over there, so for me to do the journey as soon as the weather became clement, would be more sensible. I insisted he find out my father's army number to ensure we both had the same Leslie Doyle. He got back to me quickly and confirmed this.

I wrote letters to each of my brothers for whom Bart gave me addresses and I enclosed photos of my small family.

On Saturday, 24 April 1999, Robert and I departed from Gatwick, stopping briefly at Montreal for refuelling, and arrived in Toronto, Canada, to be met by my brother Bart and Alice, who took us straight back to their home. We eventually got to bed at 11 p.m. their time, 4 a.m. ours.

There were no tears at our meeting, no emotional hugging, it was not how I'd imagined from TV programs that I've seen about this eureka moment, or as I wanted it to be, but there you have it, I was with them and time would tell whether we would form a bond and whether that would last. I had been told by Alice at the start there would be no family party, so once again, I was let down temporarily with a bump.

What she meant was that we and the three brothers and all their families would not be having a joint knees up, but she did her best and we did have meals with her family and the other brothers separately, but not *en masse*. Well that was fine by me.

On Sunday, 25 April, we went to the local Catholic church with Bart and Alice. We didn't have to, but I'd told them I'd like to fit in with their routine. They owned a small part of one of the islands which we went to see afterwards. Then we met other members of the family at their own houses, their grown-up daughters Carrie and Sally, and concluded by visiting Bart's three rental units. He gave the impression that he was a considerate landlord. Carrie is forceful and outgoing in a friendly way. She loves dragons and did or still does jigsaws of them, displaying them in frames on her walls afterward. Sally is soft and gentle and likes New Age things. After a steak supper and cinnamon pie, I spoke to my brother Jake on the phone. We all had a lot of talking to do.

On the 26th we spotted their blue jays and black squirrels, a wild cat brought her young within viewing distance, amongst other things, and we then went to the Rideau Canal and Fort Henry. Canadian robins, we discovered, are much larger than ours. We saw the former family hotel and watched my father and his wife on an old video. Bea, Sally's daughter, came to eat with us; we helped cook chilli and finished up with grapefruit.

Bart and Alice do not see their son often. All three brothers' children have had broken relationships like me. Bart is softly spoken, gentle, kind and very conscientious. He cooked a bit, and drove us everywhere even though we offered to hire a car. They did absolutely as much as they could for us. They drew their water from their own well and we could smell the sulphur; Bart had rectified that by the time we returned for a second visit.

Tuesday, 27 April, we went over on the ferry to Wolfe Island for lunch. I saw red-shouldered hawks which enthralled me. You could see the American shores from here.

On day five we treated Bart and Alice to a meal at The Red Lobster Restaurant and drove parallel to the Thousand Islands – they fascinated me.

Thursday, 29 April was industrious. We went to the

laundrette with them and we two women had our hair done. They asked me if I wanted a bang and I couldn't recall what it was at the time. We looked around town and took photos. Carrie's two daughters came to see us at supper.

On day seven we departed again, to visit Jake and have dinner with him and his wife. She seemed a little unusual, but had butterfly motifs on her jeans which I liked. Then Jake and I left the others and he proceeded to fill me in about his father whom he clearly hadn't liked. He split no hairs and if I had been a counsellor to him I couldn't have done a better job of listening and consoling, but it didn't help me any, I have to say. Jake is artistic I was told, making wooden objects and painting them to sell, just like I was in that way. He bought second-hand goods to resell and could turn his hand to anything, similar to Bart. But Jake has a trailer at a campsite where he stays for most of the summer loving the outdoors akin to me.

Leaving there we went to Niagara where Bart and Alice had ready a huge surprise for us, having booked us into a motel nearby where we had a queen-size bed (I'd not had that before). We had a cosy family evening meal together in their restaurant.

Saturday, 1 May after breakfast, we went to see the falls and it was amazing. I held my breath whilst watching the seemingly slow motion of voluminous water tumbling tirelessly down from a great height; it was mesmerizing. I said, 'I'm not going on that,' when I saw the *Maid of the Mist* floundering in the waves beneath.

'Oh yes you are,' came Bart's voice behind me. We donned the supplied rain coats and oh my, I'm glad he made me do it, it was great.

We arrived at Clive's after eating en route from Niagara where he lived with his wife. They took us off to a water-front Legion Club where there was karaoke. That was fun. Bart and Alice stayed for a night before leaving us to go back home. We'd bought Bart a T-shirt on the journey there, at a petrol station, saying, 'I like the job, it's the work I hate.' Clive seemed fierce and large, but I saw right through him. He was conscientious at helping his wife care for us and a gentle soul. We got along fine after a while.

On Sunday, 2 May, day nine, Clive took us out in his truck with his much-loved music playing loudly on the radio, then to the local casino and on to an Indian trading post. We returned to meet their adult daughter and we all had a roast dinner together. It was sad to say goodbye to Bart and Alice as we adjusted to Clive and Meg.

On day ten we met Meg's daughter from her previous marriage, with her partner; he was a loveable rogue. She had her daughter (who was fifteen at the time) with her. We went down to Lake Couchiching – how I love these names. Clive and I strode ahead as he wanted again to drive home the fact that we had an awful father and I had been better off in England without him. He pulled no punches either.

Returning to their house I found that I had been given flowers by the three girls, which was very touching. We came in from the porch after a chat for a nice family supper together. They had a little Pomeranian dog who was all over us most of the time.

On Tuesday, 4 May, I had a visit from their recycle lady who was dying to meet an English person. I bought light binoculars for all the bird spotting we were doing, most of the day was pleasantly spent by the waterfront and at the local gift shops. We had T-bone steaks for supper with Clive and Meg.

On Wednesday, 5 May, I learned there was a skunk about after questioning the strange smell on the perimeters. We went out to buy Meg some nice plants for her window boxes, then Clive left Robert and me at Lake Simcoe, where we saw a woodpecker, kingfisher and chipmunks in Provincial Park. When Clive returned at the agreed time he was surprised to find us waiting for him, saying his daughter would have kept him hanging around. I replied that if he was driving us, it was the least we could do. It was extremely hot – 83 degrees Fahrenheit or 25 degrees Centigrade – and very dry. This reminds me that Clive came into our room one morning to top up our cold drinks supply (beers, cokes) and he remarked that he was very impressed because if it had been his family they would have cleaned him out. We hadn't touched any of these, not realising they were for us but I don't believe we would have taken advantage anyway. I was also very interested in their central vacuuming system which appears to be very common in Canada.

On day thirteen we went to Lake Bass. The birds were shy at this picnic park but we could hear a number of different calls. We walked a while until we came to the cemetery where my father's grave was and I placed flowers on it and thought, *now I've caught up with you, you devil, you are still so near yet so far!* We took photos and had a McDonald's lunch across the road adjacent to a Wal-Mart where we bought silver belt buckles with eagles and wolves on them. Then Clive came to collect us.

In the evening we returned to the Legion Club again for drinks with Meg's side of the family. The men played snooker and pool. Clive was interested to know if my husband was willing to learn the refrigeration business as he needed some family member to pass it on to. Robert said no, kindly. It was then offered to Meg's daughter's partner. What a good-natured family.

I saw a cardinal singing on this last night, a nice parting gift. Bart and Alice phoned to bid us bon voyage.

Friday, 7 May. Words echo now in my head of one of the last times that Mother and I walked up Mayfield High Street, Sussex, where she finally lived in sheltered accommodation, a quarter of an hour's drive away from me. I was insistent that she tell me how to find father's family, she and I knew there was not much time left. I got angry with her for insisting it was not my business as nothing ever seems to be, it's always other peoples families, never mine. She called out as I walked away, 'What if you find something you don't like? What if one of them's been in trouble? What if you find you are not the only girl?' The last phrase didn't bother me, but the rest I suppressed.

But now I am thinking, my poor Canadian family, had they fared any better than me? I pondered over their fresh disclosures to me.

We spent Friday morning packing and Robert helped Meg's daughter sort out a computer problem. We stopped with Clive and Meg for what they called hot sandwiches on the way back to the airport. She was tearful which caught me off guard. I was happy to know she had liked my stay, but concerned for her as she suffered very bad health. We bought ourselves a wolf picture at the airport – I love wolves, my eldest granddaughter does too. We boarded the plane at 12 midnight and alighted at the next midday and I wondered where the night had gone. Robert had convinced himself he would never sleep on a plane but it was very exhausting to sit beside a constantly shifting person when I could have slept.

That was a journey taken on a 'need-to-know' basis. I will never regret it and am glad to have them.

MY BUTTERBOX SISTER!

After finding my brothers in 1999 and visiting them for the first time, I received a phone call from the eldest, Bart, telling me that he had something rather interesting to relate and would I be interested in being put in touch with a sister!

Of course after the initial surprise sank in I agreed and Mandy contacted me on 27 February 2000. She was absolutely delighted to learn about me and disappointed, she said, to have missed me on my first visit to Canada. She had been talking to my brother on a regular basis previously but still not in the guise of a sister until he imparted to her that he had just had a visit from his sister in England. At that the bubble burst, she exploded with delight declaring that she had always wanted a sister, that in fact she was his sister also and was not the genealogist she had claimed to be and could she please be put in contact with me.

I have in a letter to me, sent by my sister, an account which was written by her in 1993 for a newsletter and published in 1999 in Halifax, Nova Scotia. Mandy was born on 17 September 1939 in Nova Scotia and was cared for by her birth mother for only six months. She was at that time called Judith but then she was taken to the well-known Ideal Maternity Home where she was boarded for three months (a profile online says four).

The home was run by the Youngs, Lila (or Lela) and William. Mandy relates that she was in a very bad way due to maltreatment and even bore a life-threatening birthmark defect. This was a definite downside when the baby was presented to prospective adoptive parents. These poor babies would then allegedly be deliberately deprived of proper nutrition and upon death would be buried in a butter box duly lined with satin, hence the name, 'Butterbox Babies'.

Mandy's mother had apparently signed an elaborate contract, as did all unweds, part of which required that the adoptive parents were never to be disturbed.

Fortunately, Mandy was adopted about three months later by visiting prospectors who took pity on her.

But she implored her adoptive family, after she reached the age of thirty, to allow her some insight into her birth heritage. At this her father eventually agreed to visit a courthouse in the town where she had grown up. It had been said that the Ideal Home records had been destroyed in a fire when the building was burnt to the ground in 1962 but, as luck would have it, the clerk managed to produce them and her mother's name and address were procured from the documents. The search moved on to her mother's home village and enquiries were made at the local post office.

Being told that her birth mother had moved away, they clutched at the straw that her mother had a sister nearby and they ventured on.

After much ado the sister finally agreed to approach Mandy's birth mother and ask if she could see her, but she stipulated that communication would be via Mandy's adoptive parents.

It wasn't until after three years of successfully receiving the desired information that Mandy plucked up the courage to contact Parent Finders to ask if they would make the initial phone call for her.

Eventually she met and shared two days with her birth mum swapping stories and pictures I am told.

Of a natural course Mandy wanted to know about her biological father too. She was told by her mother that he was a Roman Catholic and married when she met him. Her mother was hurt, bitter and defensive after being unmarried (with the entire attached stigma) and having to part with a child, she was also reluctant to impart much more about Mandy's father. But after some years she relented and details were extracted.

Mandy searched in the National Archives of Ottawa (available at local libraries) and found his name. Again taking the advice of Parent Finders she wrote him an open letter using the excuse, she says, that she was trying to create a family tree, but did not say she was his daughter. She got the old age security pension department to forward it to him.

A meeting was arranged and she and her husband visited him. She learned that she had three half-brothers at this point, one of which she later talked to on the phone using genealogy as her excuse again.

Incidentally she stated that our father and brother never asked her where she fitted on the family tree.

In this particular case, once being able to claim herself finally successful in tracking her past, Mandy was happy to carry on with her much-loved adoptive family as her own, which as I write now in 2006 is quite extensive. I have recent photos of them all, she sees no need to experience life any further with her birth ties, this I can understand and am happy for her and with her in exclaiming that she truly has 'a complete past'.

Mandy has visited me in England and stayed for two weeks. Her daughter Joan accompanied her for a while and then went off on a tour of England and Scotland. I am happy that we email quite frequently, which fills in a gap for both of us at times I hope.

It is amazing to think that during all those years of my

searching for my father, she was accomplishing these things too. I do not have a lot in common with her apart from the fact that she adores music like me, we are both outgoing now (I previously wasn't) and that with regard to our roots – we both needed to know!

A point of interest is that she had three children with her husband in quick succession then after a few years adopted a fourth, Joan 'as pay back', she told me. What a lovely thing to do, because the last is as much her own as the others, I know this as a fact. She has helped her adopted daughter to do her own search also once she was ready, this included meeting her birth mother too, a generous act on Mandy's behalf.

I am so sad to say that just recently Mandy's lovely daughter Joan died of cancer, leaving two little ones and a beloved husband. Joan was only thirty-eight years of age and Mandy's message to all of us is to regularly check our moles in case of melanomas.

PARADIGM SHIFT

Thomas Kuhn devised a theory called paradigm shift which, simply explained, has the meaning that old ideas or methods are ousted by new inclusions, causing a crisis and then new beginnings.

I have learned never to take no for an answer, because living with insubstantial evidence always points to more possibilities thus I carry with me the determination never to accept defeat at any turn of the road or stage of my life. I needed to draw on that strength to relay to you this next part of my story.

This most awful part of my life which I have not yet dealt with and which screams like that invisible, ever-present elephant to be noticed, is my first marriage. I want to say that without it I would not have my two lovely sons, so there's a positive, the only one I'm afraid.

We first met at Peggy Spencer's School of Dancing in Crystal Palace, Sydenham, Kent. I fell in love with him at first sight. He asked me to dance with him, but I later heard that he did so in order to ask me to ask my best friend at that time, Lynda, to go out with his best friend. This friend was watching eagerly from the edge of the dance floor for some sign of success and my agreement. But that didn't transpire. Hugo and I danced slowly together for some time. I had never felt like that, swooning with our young first love and amazement. He asked me to meet him at the cinema in the near future and I accepted at once.

He was always playing tricks, like altering his watch to pretend I was a few minutes late which in fact I never was, being a conscientious person. He sang songs like 'Do Not Forsake Me Oh My Darling'. There was no fear of that. He joked about a little black book which he kept to write any misdemeanours in, when he felt I'd upset him, usually some silly little thing, like not noticing something about him for instance. We used to skip across the zebra crossings avoiding the white lines, singing, 'This is my song, my very own song, I can sing it short or I can sing it long,' with a chorus of, '*lah de da, de da, etc, la de dah de dum dum*'. We seemed so childishly happy.

I loved him so much; he was my idol, my long-awaited white knight. My heart skipped a beat when he came to the door, and was torn from me at each departure.

The trouble was a lot of other women felt the same way about him. I started to have them approach me when I was out, to stake a claim. Anonymous callers were always phoning me right up to the day he left. He was systematically breaking my heart. We'd courted from when I was fifteen and he sixteen for five years and I feel he only may have asked me to marry him because my mother had a go at him, and due to additional compulsions of outside pressure.

We had to live with his parents at first, which was a nightmare for me, for as kind as anyone intends to be it never really works out. Then they found us a flat with a close friend of theirs who reported back our every move and always to the negative. I felt imprisoned. Hugo found a house in Tunbridge Wells and we briefly stayed with his parents again in Beckenham, Kent, with no time to ourselves, while the last leg of the house went up.

I became pregnant with Jack who was born in 1965 and we moved into our brand new house in Lambourne Way, Tunbridge Wells, Kent. My dreams were soon disintegrated as I found out that my beloved husband was never going to be present, even though we had now achieved the dream of our own beautiful home and child. Not being there when I gave birth – he, my mother informed me, was at a party – or when the first baby, Jack, was young and sickly, I had to struggle by myself to get to the doctor and to administer medicines without any support. A frightening, lonely existence for one who'd had no experience of the family nucleus. He said he was always working, but word got back that he was playing hard and in mixed company, often at the horse races and afterward partying.

This is what led to me becoming depressed and my doctor prescribing medication. I received Valium, Librium and sleeping tablets, responding like a robot to daily requirements in order to cope with my husband's disloyal treatment of me. Even our next-door neighbour approached him and said, 'You have a beautiful young wife, she really loves you and wants to be with you,' to no effect. I spent a short while in Amberstone Hospital in East Sussex as I was thinking about harming myself in my misery, but I discharged myself when I finally saw sense and dropped all the medication, albeit against professional advice. I witnessed people who'd had electric shocks as treatment going 'doolally' and others locked away in Hellingly (part of the same complex but for really disturbed patients) who had gone mad. I soon got out of there, but not without learning compassion for those lost souls. I had to find mine!

I tried to pick up the pieces and we moved again to a bungalow in Strawberry Close, bordering on Tunbridge Wells in Frant, Sussex. An upgrade to increase his assets he told me. This property should have been like an unbelievably grand experience, but having received a phone call and visit from one of his women who he'd had at least one child with and with my knowledge bought a home for on the South Coast, this was not so. I was carrying my second child in my womb, so I hardly saw it that way.

It is strange that in this new area, my second husband's uncle at one time resided just a few doors away from me. His name was Percy Barden and he had been mayor of Maidstone, and was a leading home builder in that part of the world. The property's previous owner, Mr Brickman, had befriended us and the boys used his swimming pool in the summer, at one time he bought Jack a Tottenham Hotspur football outfit, as he was on the team's committee. Are we to believe that my next husband's uncle was put there perhaps as a signpost or stepping stone, pointing forward, on some psychic level? The memory of him was that he owned two beautiful cars – a Jaguar and a Rolls Royce – and he had his initials on the number plates PAB (Percy Albert Barden).

Of our home I reminisce that it backed onto forest land belonging to the Marquis of Abergavenny and we had badgers roaming there at night and foxes calling. I remember Sheba, our Alsatian, dashing out into the night to try and track them down. Jack loved horse riding at this time, and ventured through the forest on horseback, with a riding school which I kept up for him as long as I could afford to. He also attended a private school for a short while.

Both of these had to end when Hugo left.

My sons have grown to be fruitful. The youngest, Alex, has evolved to be a film and media teacher and has his own little company. He has a nice Thai wife, but suffers ill health at times.

Jack is doing well working for a telecom company and has his own website where he uses the internet as a gathering place for all levels of chess players. He has a supportive wife and two lovely daughters.

THE TURNAROUND
– ONE DOOR CLOSING

My crumbling world gave way after many serious rows. As previously said, I'd been pregnant with my second child at the time of the other woman's visit. Alex was born in 1972 and later diagnosed as an asthmatic; this was unfortunate as he would need help at a time when I really needed to be caring for myself. Hugo and I subconsciously knew this was the end, and he eventually went to yet another woman and I had major decisions to make.

The solicitor I had hired for the divorce advised me that it was accepted law that I could stay at the bungalow until the youngest reached eighteen or make my own way with the remaining equity. Hugo had warned me not to use a solicitor otherwise he wouldn't help me however I carried on regardless.

I obtained a quick divorce, as I could see no point in prolonging the agony and keeping a bird who'd already flown the cage, apart from the fact that I'd long ago decided I did not want to remain with an unfaithful person and lose my little remaining self-respect. My decision resulted in me having to sell the bungalow, paying half the profit to him after the mortgage was paid off. I bought a small house with the change, in Jarvis Brook, Crowborough, Sussex. It had a tiny garden and only storage heaters, all I could afford.

I had Sheba, the Alsatian, put down, as she was used to a third of an acre of garden with open-gated access to the forest behind and me having plenty of time to walk her. Not to mention the expense of keeping a large dog.

Jack remembers the story of when at Strawberry Close, ignoring my warning, he rode on her back, fell off and fractured his collarbone. His own fault entirely.

I recollect that on one sailing holiday in Devon, Sheba swam out after us when we were heading for a friend's boat and I had to return to shore beside her in the dingy. She was so loyal that she swam back with me, while the rest of the family and friends carried on out in the row boat to the vessel and waiting sea. At Strawberry Close and our previous home in Lambourne Way, she and our black moggie Fluff (Jack named her) used to bundle together in play fights and were a joy to behold. We went together to dog training classes. It was a sad loss when Sheba was gone.

I found a job in Crowborough. It was difficult working firstly as a waitress, then as a school supervisor and being a one-parent family. I needed to top up the small maintenance Hugo allowed us. I had my final divorce papers, but we haggled for years as I tried to get a decent amount from him to support his boys. That was never forthcoming although what we did receive was paid regularly.

I discarded the time-wasting solicitors and represented myself in court in order to obtain Alex's first aeroplane flight and holiday in Italy with Robert and me. I won the case. When he was younger he had been away with the school but only via a ferry.

Fortunately, the Thatcher government brought in some assistance for one parent families around that time, which I appreciated as a small help with day-to-day existence.

Instead of dragging the whole of my story through the mud and grime, I'll ask you to picture the previous disclosures punctuated through with intervals of snowstorms and icicles, lightning and thunder. Imagine a severed, bloodied heart pounded with unrelenting rains.

The trouble is, this is a simple form of sketching out my life with Hugo and the trial which I was continually facing. I yearned in vain for this man to be part of my life; clearly our planets were out of alignment and we were continually battered by magnetic storms!

Now insert an image of my mother appearing in sporadic sessions that intervene in our married life, complaining about gossip she'd heard in relation to the infidelity that I am presently protesting about. I had been continually delivering anguished onslaughts to Hugo regarding this, which he constantly denied. She did not aid me in my situation, but compounded it. I can understand it hurt her to stand by helplessly watching me suffer.

In the famous song 'Achy Breaky Heart' by Billy Ray Cyrus, reason goes out the window and at the time (the song says) it might 'blow up and kill this man'. One might feel this way and it takes time to move on from the person who's left you in this heartbroken state.

A great, dark void spanned in front of me and a tortured soul agonised every time another woman claimed him from the previous one, reliving its hurt as I do, and the sorrow of all his waiting children, hoping for scraps of attention from this rich man's table. Yes rich in money, but as yet no evidence have I seen of him being rich with a genuine, generously offered love.

I am left with a vision of two little boys sitting on a bottom stair waiting for the phone to ring because their father did not turn up. The voice on the phone will say in its detached way that Dad is sorry but has been detained again today and perhaps we can do it another time. Would that not wrench a poor mother's heart?

My sons may not like me to tell this story, but it is my story, equivalent to my divulging the facts I do about Mother too which belong to my story. I'm owning it at last, but for the first time. I will not be prevented again by fear from telling it, because other people may express their discomfort for what I'm saying. If that is the case then I'm sorry, but it needs to be done.

I will take my leave from this topic at this juncture. Hugo has now set up home with a new partner who, I found, was on the scene at the start when he began his business in Surrey. Curiously, I later learned that when I was having our first child within wedlock his mistress, who had visited me had just had hers in their seaside abode.

I cannot understand why people look up to statures such as these. My first husband, Hugo, was admired by many people, who always said that he has a charming man. I was also told that people often said the same about my father. They seemed to be looking up to the wrong people! I have always found that hard to accept, especially when those in the English parliament lead double lives whilst having responsible positions. Men like this hurt many innocent people, especially those who leave children fatherless. I try not to be too judgemental, but it's a feeling I can't discard yet; maybe I never will, as I am one of those walking in the deserted child's moccasins.

I have not slated my first husband or slandered his character beyond what is truthful, my boys could ask no more than that. Jack keeps in touch with him; Alex chooses not to at present. I did the best I could for them and ask forgiveness for my short temper when, like my mother, I was driven to distraction with unhappiness and fear for our future.

After a few years alone with the boys, I met my present husband with whom I strived to achieve the longed-for family unit. Knitting together ill-fitting, sensitive individuals with lost and damaged pasts was a long and difficult task as I'm sure many people in my position can vouch for. But I think we got there in the end. The boys will have their own stories as will their stepfather.

QUITE A CHARACTER

I will describe Mother's character now as only I can and as it occurs to me.

She had a sense of humour and she loved to sing.

I remember songs like, 'Oh my Darling Clementine', 'You are my Sunshine', and 'Under the Spreading Chestnut Tree'. She also taught me 'Frère Jacques' and other French songs which is how I knew some French. She would smile while she sang and wave her bony hand with clenched fist and extended forefinger about as if conducting an orchestra. This same finger would often preach vindictively to me. She was a slight, diligent, hard-working soul. Maybe that is where I got that character trait from, but I use it in the mental sense whilst she exercised it mainly in the physical.

Until her dying day she appreciated nature, loving lambs in the fields, birds singing, bright flowers and the ducks on a pond – all simple pleasures. She saved hard and went without a lot of things which she could afford in her later life but was fearful of buying in case she lived too long and ran out of money.

She enthused over second-hand statues, a typically blue-and-white Dutch boy and girl for instance, or a fawn-coloured bambi fixed to a flower vase. Many a time she'd hasten to a flea market and then return home proudly to display some figurine, which she felt sure she'd struck a good bargain for. One could never convince her that an old coal scuttle box, for example, wouldn't be worth a fortune, it was more than our life was worth.

She could compete with the best when stating facts about football, the players and the results of the last games. My boys had many pleasant hours discussing this subject with her and watching the matches. Her knowledge of card games was extensive and Jack and Alex enjoyed visiting as it always involved the experience of learning new tricks, especially exciting at Christmas when we all played for coppers.

Where she got her love of politics from I will never know, but she was well-informed and up to date on this subject, which she felt was important. Always claiming to be a Little Englander, she said that we couldn't be beaten in the war so Brussels would get the better of us in a different way; I cannot comment on that. I wonder how she would feel about the War on Terror and all that has happened since she died in 1996.

How mother loved wearing pinks, blues, whites and lilacs. Any combination of pastel shades appealed to her. She looked very delicate in them and even attractive, although she felt she wasn't. She claimed to be a smart dresser in her youth even without much money and remained neat and tidy until her dying day. The hairdresser came to her flat in her last days, when she could no longer get out. Her eyesight was always bad, therefore I never saw her without glasses. She loved costume jewellery and was never seen without a chain of pearl or crystal beads around her neck and little clip-on earrings.

Her hands were rough and worn from the lifelong toil. She wore the engagement ring from my first dissolved marriage, which I gave her from the goodness of my heart because no one had ever given her a ring. She declared that she would never give it back to me, even if I asked, now that she had it.

Her back was stooped into a dowager's hump, she ached

from arthritis most of the time and was painfully thin, I want to say from constant worrying, but am sure that was not the only reason, for she undoubtedly lacked nutrition in her formative years. Mum was excellent at plain, good, home cooking, and we all loved her roast dinners. There was always plenty on the plate and it was delicious. She'd sit for hours doing her crossword puzzles and was pleased with herself because it gave her some self-esteem to be able to say she could easily do them. It kept her mind active, that I can say.

Her hair remained very dark until quite late in life when it took on an attractive grey/blue hue and, as previously mentioned, she'd worn false teeth from the time I was twelve.

She was reluctant to talk badly about her mother and father even though she'd been taken away from them in Guernsey and sent to England to be put into a foster home due to their lack of regard for her, the eldest of twelve. Mother once told me in a weak moment that she remembers sitting in a room when she was little and there was absolutely no furniture on the floors nor any furnishings on the walls or at the window, it was completely bare. She admitted she was mischievous when young, but that left me thinking yes, but if you can be, then why not me?

From the age of about seventy she'd continually say she wanted to die and that made me feel awful, but when the time came she told me that she'd called out for me because she knew Lesley would do something to help her when the nurses had told her to be quiet because she wasn't the only one in the hospital. Fancy waiting until your last two days before you realise that the one who would help you the most sincerely was the person who'd been constantly at your side but you'd been putting down!

If only she could have dropped her guard and shared her secrets with me, I'm sure we could have hugged each other and nothing more would have stood between us.

LIVING UNDER THE LIE

Here I'd like to ask you, the reader, how would you feel if after living for sixty-four years you suddenly came to the realisation, that for fifty-six of them, you had been living under a lie?'

Just think about that for a moment.

Would you trust anyone ever again after being so misled, for so long?

Would you believe in anything, after finding your whole life history and summary of experiences dissolved before your eyes and taking on a new meaning, in other words, the curriculum vitae of your entire existence and function invalid, unfaithful and crossed out?

But the astonishing fact was that Mother was the whole time laying down new codes of conduct for me to follow, on top of her own old codes of deception. She enacted sweet and sour contrasts upon my senses, because whatever she underlined for me as her unquestionable spoken truth, would always be questioned by my underlying silent self feeling that something was off, never quite right. No words could be put to it, but I wasn't swallowing the ruse although my thinking mind did not speak its doubts regarding her accounts to me, therefore rendering itself to living in denial of that buried data with no self discovery map for location purposes, enough to blow someone's mind I would say!

I had to be perfect. Yet, however blameless I was, the dark shadow nevertheless still hung over me. Following her directions was unprosperous for me, but critically important in her view that I must adhere to this flawless discipline. Being compressed into shape by following rules which allowed others to constantly observe and monitor my robotic actions doesn't allow for a lot of free thinking, so I escaped and expanded my imagination on the invisible plane, unnoticed. I was living two lives, the most fruitful of which was to use intuition to discover new things and stay out of danger as animals do. I was just a child, how pitiable.

So when it happened that I, in adulthood, found my Canadian family, the horrible news that they gave me jolted me into trying to figure out which world of these two parallel choices would be best for me to inhabit: England and Mother's false version, or Canada and the brothers' true account of history. Then of course, there was my own imaginative world if push came to shove, but that wasn't really a serious option.

Do you believe the truth is best for everyone regardless of what it may do to them? The impact can be as devastating as the biblical flood, but after a settling period I decided that there was nothing quite like the truth and this I could not change and so I would stick with its relative solidarity.

A new spin was applied to my life and now the English girl chose to live out her Canadian side for a change. The illegitimate black sheep became a love child. The woman without family would claim her remote siblings, a birth receipt must be transformed to a full certificate if possible, the incomplete evidence to be transfigured into positive DNA proof, a half-person into a whole.

While I was ill and at one time partially bedridden I now maintain better health than ever before. I claim to be happier and humbly stating that I am progressively working to add to my capacity for knowledge. Some may consider me eccentric but my improved drive – due to freed up, recycled energy accelerates me more successfully beyond the normal plagues of everyday life, due partly to the fact that it is more conducive to one's affairs if we can detach from keeping up with the Joneses or conforming to other people's views.

Now the second of my two main goals looms ahead, for I am one, remember, who had a severely interrupted education, moving around as we did and hurried into the market place at first chance. I want the opportunity to publish my own story, my first book.

I woke up this morning with the phrase, 'The best things in life are free', running through my head. OK it's a saying of the poor maybe, but I was brought up in the main part of my childhood years by the coast, where I had a rich abundance of time to harvest natural play within the landscape of the untamed, sun, sand and the sea, lucky me. I feel that I have a mind of my own!

OLD SELF DIES FIRST

This would not be a proper representation of my life without relaying my encounter with the Light.

There is a film called *Touch of Hope* which is based on a true happening. A man witnesses a horrific accident and, upon cradling the dreadfully injured victim in his arms and experiencing some power or light emanating from or through him to her, finds later that she has been released prematurely from hospital relatively unharmed. This was one of many incidents and he began to feel alien to people around him. He tried to get them to see where he was coming from, and they continually provoked him for dropping his mundane affairs to tend to his weird (as they saw it) newfound unprovable ability. This insight and gift took over and he was naturally enraptured by it. His surroundings fell to ruins and his progress into this new awareness continued as he disappeared from their view, allegorically speaking, and embarked on the voyage to enlarge his knowledge of it and even to try and discover a way to convert the sceptics.

I do not have the gift to heal, I hasten to say, but I have poignant memories which touched me as I viewed the Light!

In physics a structural failure happens when the load carrying capacity breaks down, after reaching critical mass and deformations occur. Thermal shock results in major cracks as the temperature or temperaments of members have reached their limits as I had reached mine.

I was sick of the world; it was not one I was proud to belong to or be part of. Stress had caused my limbs to become set and weak and I could hardly get myself about.

Then there was a large gathering in church for one purpose in March 1988, the day of repentance. I had always believed in God and was kneeling and praying for the world along with the congregation, expecting something to happen. After a period of silence I heard this ringing in my head. Looking up through my hands, unaware of my surroundings I saw a glowing, amazing shower of brilliant white light and a dazzling star expanding before me, consisting of this same white ambience emerging in so many rays like the sun. Next from the right came the most beautiful, mischievous-looking face beaming at me full of warmth, play and lovingness. I was transfixed, as it travelled across my vision and was clothed in light, rose up and then it fixed me with its gaze of piercing eyes. I felt changed in an instant and thought, *it must be real; it feels warm and is friendly*. Everything will be all right it conveyed, and it told me to look for the good: 'It's in the shape of an arch.' I felt a lot of energy but was not afraid of its presence. I did not understand that last phrase at the time! Then it veered off again to the right from whence it came and I came round in a confused state to the sounds of the gathering singing 'Bind us together Lord, bind us together Lord, with cords that can never be broken' I will never forget those words.

At this point I felt we could all stop praying because the future was taken care of, our efforts had not been in vain and my heart was pounding. I tried desperately to tell my husband, but he had not been taken up in this manner although he was right beside me. I wrote a letter afterward to the church and they said that some others present had had similar experiences.

It did not stop there however and it was at this point that

I found the courage to dispense with my solicitors and I went to represent myself in court and won.

Gradually my small insignificant consciousness began to expand, subjects previously unknown to me began to unfold and I knew something incredible was happening to me. I felt I was being taught by teachers invisible. I tried my hand at painting and poetry. I began getting messages, but frighteningly they conveyed facts about incidents that had not happened, then at intervals planes crashed to the ground, and other occurrences took place. I was appalled. My frustration was that the messenger said I must tell no one. I have since learned that this was a safeguard against my infancy in this experience, which I felt an urgent need to tell about, but try as I might, no one understood me anyway. What on earth was going on?

As years have gone by I have accessed websites on the subject of spiritual ascension leading towards 2012 and have found solace there. Nowhere else on the physical plane can I find a person on my level of consciousness; that is lonely. Yet I have my spirit person or soulmate constantly talking to me, so I am not really alone. I marvel daily at its communication with me and I wouldn't exchange it for anything in the world.

I believe, as a knock-on effect from this, the means were given to me and my husband to find my brothers and ultimately gain my father's name upon my birth certificate. I began to notice synchronicities in my life.

Near-death experiences or related phenomena are not uncommon nowadays, websites are full of them. If we are laden with regrets, and with the same old patterns occurring frequently, the postponement of dealing with them hampers our enjoyment of a transformed future.

Contrariwise, could it be the right-hand brain's abrupt evolution with its associated insight and intuition, coming to assist the left, its brother, which is bound to tedious, analytic intellectualism?

JUDGEMENT DAY

I arrived at court in Tunbridge Wells on 9 October 2006 fully expecting to see the same judge again, only to be informed that today it would be a different one. I worked at not letting this upset me mentally as I waited to go into his chambers.

This was the final hearing and my heart was far from steady. Not only was the decision going to be final but this date here in England coincided with Canada's Thanksgiving Day, which seemed somewhat eerie and special to me although I felt I should be getting used to odd happenings by now.

Judge McLoghlin eventually had me summoned and bade me sit down. He then explained that I would swear an oath on the Bible to tell the truth and then he would write in freehand then read off into his tape recording machine my responses as he questioned me about them.

He said that the most important pieces of evidence were my mother's word of mouth during her life to me, the affidavit, the letters of contact between my Canadian family and me, and the DNA results. He read a lot of clauses and subclauses that meant nothing to me. I was a bit nervous as I had been asked by the clerk before entering the judge's room who was representing me. I answered that I was, because my solicitor had rightly said that no one would ever be able to remember all the facts the same as myself. This gave me the feeling that my being present alone was somewhat strange and I hoped this would not impede my progress in any way.

We worked together through the identical files that I had constructed, one for his reference, the other for mine. Now Cathleen Adams' affidavit came into play as Judge McLoghlin mentioned that and her long-standing friendship with my mother. I was asked to relate the story of how my mother met my father and the details that she gave me; for example his army number and his family's hotel in Ontario. He also commented on my brother's letter stating that he believed I was his sister on account of the many facts I had given him and the family traits I possessed. The main factor of note had to be the DNA testing of course which the judge cited as positive proof therefore enabling him to pass a judgement or ruling that my father's name would be put on my birth certificate. I sighed with relief and happiness asking quickly if we could include that he belonged to the Canadian Armed Forces. 'You can have what you want,' he said calmly. I could not help thinking that if only judges were allowed to show and share jubilance with us, how great that would seem. Comments were made by him as to the effort put into the case and to what a remarkable story it was, steeped with my assembled family history.

Finally he recorded that: 'Lesley had had a long and emotional journey which became less inhibited after her mother's death in order to find her roots,' and that he found it all an exceptional and incredible story. His face softened at the end and even his eyes became watery (so they are human).

After thanking him profusely I came away to await the general form of judgement or order. This would state the court's result to the Registrar General, which has to be sent within twenty-one days of the conclusion of the case. Then they would carry out the re-registration and produce the new birth certificate. This entry would naturally show the findings of the court after verifying the information with the applicant. I cannot emphasise enough that it was mentioned several times by different people whom I encountered in the court during these procedures, that this was a most unusual case.

The declaration of parentage was dated 12 October 2006, this date being my mother's birthday, had she been here to see it!

THE GREAT SHADOW

My last thoughts when I lay down to sleep the night before writing this chapter were: please Lord, give me a way to relate this last chapter as harmlessly as possible. Below is what I was given by the next morning.

My aim is to be at peace with myself, but not to harm my surrounding environment. It is painfully obvious that I have been wounded. A pressure was exerted upon me from the start. What my mother hid from me I grew to believe was to my detriment and wielded a quiet blaming, of which I questioned, 'Was I the cause?'

After my first visit to Canada, full of excitement at the thought of meeting my freshly discovered brothers, I came back like a loaded bomber. Each of the brothers had piled what could be interpreted as explosives into my already upset stomach. Now I had been primed to detonate. Never before had I needed so urgently to part with my consignment in order to heal my wounds.

So, like the planes returning from their missions in wartime obliged to dump their load, I have to release this volatile material into the atmosphere, preferably over a derelict and expansive area, targeting no one.

I do not have much information, but here are the few facts that I have gathered from various sources.

The great shadow that had been haunting me was that my father's Division had been in the thick of the fighting in Italy for over a month when something happened that led to my father being sentenced to death by firing squad after being found guilty of murder. The judgement was eventually commuted to life imprisonment, which resulted in him being sent to a Canadian penitentiary.

In an Ottawa newspaper report that we found online, dated November 1943 and relating to the event on 6 November, it said that Father had been drinking the local vino at an Italian farmhouse, and, when he returned to camp that evening, he dozed in front of the fire, loaded rifle in hand. A sergeant approached and tried to wake the sleeping gunner. After some exchange my father shot and killed him. It then tells how my father left the tent, shot and killed another sergeant, wounded a gunner, and then attempted suicide. The court martial was held in the field in Italy on 14 and 15 June 1944, but it related only to the first incident.

This agrees roughly with how the family had told it. I must admit I was numbed for a long time finding it hard to accept that my father had done this.

I have read in one book that my father was awake and chatty, and that after a scuffle he was shot in the head. I had heard that he was shipped back to an English hospital for his operation, taking months to recover, before being returned to Canada after being given a glass eye.

Sometime after my arrival back in England I received an account of father's court case from my Canadian cousin in the colony. This again reaffirmed that father was stationed in Italy, but does not confirm whether he was drunk. It does state that he tried to kill himself after the activities recounted above and that he was probably not aware of what he was doing at the time. I understand that the court recommended mercy because the findings were not unanimous.

I naturally told my boys about the sequence of events after visiting my brothers, making very light of the main

122

points I must admit, but I had vowed to myself never to conceal items which could cause a silent block betwixt them and me as they are two of my most precious persons in my life. People should not be treated as stupid; we are fully aware of impressions exuding from each others' auras.

I once came across a North American plant called the Canadian Flea Bane, which overran England, just as the Canadian soldiers did when winning our young girl's hearts those many years ago. It's commonly known that seeds are carried in the bellies of innocent birds. This plant, like the poppy, seems to pop up through tiny cracks. In other words, can appear where you'd least expect them to thrive. Harmless looking, but a ticking time bomb.

I want to explode my time bomb now, to reduce any further devastation. The fallout should have lost its effect on those who knew for their lifetime the above disclosure. I have had seven years to acclimatise to it. It can be eradicated if we see that it falls on barren ground, not letting our past control our future.

As the media climate hots up, the type of news relayed becomes more ruthless in its reaching tendrils. There can be no more nasty secrets unearthed that belonged to my mother, or secrets remaining in me when future generations, on either side of the pond, effortlessly research their family history with the aid of progressed technology. It is normal that they would want to question. No more cloak and dagger manoeuvres.

How did you feel Mother, as I stroked your brow when you were on your death bed? When I told you how very loved you had been by me? You having been left, marooned and isolated by your own hand, taking toxins with you? How can I assuage it, unless I unveil its face, whereby proving to you in your spirit world that it is not now considered your shame, nor mine. The world has changed; it no longer judges you for being an unmarried parent of an only child with no name. You need trouble yourself no further; from now on it is put to flight forever.

Gone is the unconscious hidden ogre that I sensed in a puzzling, disturbing way, down through my lifetime of experiences. It spread its tentacles into corners, causing growing deathlike, constricting cancers.

It has hurt me immensely to write this last chapter because of the guilt I had felt in exposing it, but it had to be done, I think for the good. I have taken hold of a new broom now and its approach is to sweep clean. Mother did not want to put upon me, I'm sure, but she did by her unspoken words – unintentionally.

How Mother bore it, I shall never know; locked in combat with her mind. Sometimes she told me he was a charmer, at other times evil.

At a later date, this act of his was proven to be post-traumatic stress and he was released, but he alone bears the brunt of this in accountability, and his family can be held in no way responsible. He lived with that shame and I'm sure in hell, until 1997, one year after my mother passed away.

I must now leave her behind, having removed the dense layers of caked-on mud holding me back. Having broken that hefty shell and driven my demons out, their curse dispelled. Disabling the ghosts has been life changing. I have moved from one whose tastes were ordinary to one who enjoys travelling the fields of more varied interests, having found new ability to understand more complex subjects. I no longer feel alien to myself. I am in a more comfortable blueprint; this means recycled energy at my disposal. Growth follows where one's energy flows and this newly discovered being of mine is where I am magnetised to.

Sometimes we must work through intense pain. To be kept chained down serves no useful purpose. The scars I bear no longer infect me; my inherited, long-guarded secret is out. I have at this moment in time a fractured elbow because I tried to carry too much. This, I understand, will gradually fill in the gaps as it mends. Likewise, I am simply following nature's natural healing process. I've filled in the gaps, I am mended and my spirit is not completely broken after all.

There you are. That's my secret. This whale, now unlike the one that I compared myself to at the beginning, has navigated its own way out of the narrow, constricting channels and well-meaning, but interfering forces. I must say that I can also mildly associate with Michelangelo, in the way that the painting of his famous ceiling caused his body grief, but his spirit impelled him.

The knowledge of this incident, which explains why I suffered such a misled life, is not worth acquiring if I bottle it up again. With this visualisation exercise, the opposite of the sort I would normally practise, as it is unpleasant, I strive to give my father and I an option. I'm looking from another angle, where even angels may fear to tread, not to excuse these awful, indescribable acts, but to give him the benefit of the doubt and me an opportunity to allow for some form of compassion. So this is how I feel it might have been via his eyes, could he speak:

'I have been under constant fire all day long, for many days of which I have lost count. I don't have much more than this to look forward to. I am deafened and dulled by shells whizzing relentlessly over my head, there are dead and damaged bodies all around. The screams and the stench are sickening, intolerable. The certainty of more guns, more drudgery, more fighting, more bloody, mangled mates – it's getting me down. I operate like a piece of machinery; I cannot stand it any more. The shouts of incomings and outgoings are now customary as shuddering sounds jolt my jangled nerves, shaking the already battered earth, a hellhole with no light at the end of its tunnel. Is this my last moment? Flashes blind me, flying debris petrifies me. Will it end now? Today? Will it never end? How will it?

I gain some leave. The one thought in my mind is to head out for a drink. I am partial to wine and to its ability to dull my senses; it's the only other way I know that's close at hand. Its potency gives some relief, but then I have to steal myself. I head back sleepily, lethargically, forcing my reluctant body to return to that dreaded camp where I will be ordered to go back out again to war tomorrow. I am anxious that my mates will hold me to my promise. I am the musical one, the means for them to have a sing-song in order to lift our spirits, forget the blackness and the yearned-for folks back home. The effect will be only momentary. It always falls upon the entertainer of the group. Usually I might not mind but it's such a responsibility and today I don't want it.

I slump down by the fire in a semi-awake state. Suddenly someone says something to me. I resist their prodding. I'm not in the mood for this. Why don't they leave me alone? They are harshly nudging me back to reality against my wishes. Now I take on fight and flight responses, conditioning from the automatic reactions of the day. Those spoken words trigger a personal response in me, vital words that can never be told, because it's too late… I've had enough. I erupt, strike out blindly, thrashing about. I snap, going beyond reason, out of control. Half mad, unaware, still drowsy, up comes my gun – *bang, bang, bang* – no time to weigh up what I am doing. I point it straight at my head. Who cares? I just want out of this ugly world, I just want to die. *Bang!* Darkness… am I dead?'

Musical people – and I've been told that he liked to play the showman – tend to be volatile and sensitive, vulnerable to being pushed over the edge. He must also have held a lot of locked-up suppression, it doesn't take a genius to work that out. The picture above, however unreliable, is the way I have preferred to understand, remember and put it to bed. It

was long ago and anything recurring and limiting reduces
our power to change.

EPILOGUE

In January 2007 I attended a Progressive Personal Awareness course at West Kent College, Tonbridge, Kent. In one of the exercises we had to depict ourselves as a hero-like character in a well known story. I decided to be Hiawatha as I felt akin to him, being similarly brought up alone with one guardian and, like him, loving wildlife and nature. The main reason however that I chose to associate my life with his was that he confronted his father, the west wind, Mudjeekeewis, who had deserted his mother leaving her with child. This gave me a way of dealing with this similar circumstance although I could only confront my father in visualisation. The following is my retelling of the story.

Introduction:
On the bank of a river stood Flies with a Broken Wing, an Indian brave. On the other side of the river stood the place his eyes must evade, a place where his heart longs to go, and proves to be the place of his destiny, across the wide, fierce expanse, denied to him many moons ago, and he tells his story.

The following should be read in the style of the epic poem *Hiawatha* by Henry W Longfellow:

Once I journeyed onward, upward, left my family, friends behind me, left the world I knew and crossing, to a shore, I knew not of it, over to forbidden places, travelling where taboos forbade me, past the scolding hands that pointed, past the wagging tongues negating, came upon a rocky highway to his kingdom, my dead father, where, upon the gusty summits, faced the truth about his misdeeds, whence committing wrongful actions, filled with anger causing terror, all these aspects and deception, hanging in the air with wildness, tossed about, these shameful conducts gleaming from the eyes of brothers, falsehoods poisoning each the other, quarrels they could not forgive him, like a sky filled black with thunder.

So I raged unto my father, you have killed my mother's spirit, taken all her youth, her whole life, broken pieces are my brothers, trampled hopes and dreams beneath you, you are guilty, you are guilty, and he waved his fist unto me, tossed his head in great contempt, then he anguished, had misgivings, bowed his head and then consented, bowed his head and once relented. We thus held a deadly conflict, wearing plumes and waving war clubs, far away in distant places, 'cross that wide and threatening river, high upon those looming mountains, cold and icy, capped and snowy, where the ghosts and all the shadows, run the pathways 'cross the heavens, crowded with the trace of memories, vapoured mists conceal their presence, but believe me they are watching, just believe me they are seeing.

In confusion of the battle, in the shoutings and the clashing, he conveyed his awful message, that his actions were immortal, now engraved in every memory, writings carved in stone the outcome. I so brave to seek his presence, have to face that it is written, cannot change his deeds so dreadful, can't erase his reputation, must accept that revelation, so I come back from my journey, not defeated but the wiser, having done my great adventure, freshly killed that awful dragon, having that success to build on, bravely gained the strength to live on.

Heedless of my broken wing I continue singing,
Seen, the angels close above, toward them I am winging.

130

Joyful as the uplift flowers' blue skies their intention,
Guiding my undying hearts' enchanted spirit
strengthened…

This name, Flies with a Broken Wing, is a name I feel I have
earned.

Appendix / Synchronicity

Synchronicity

8 September 1942:	when I was born, birthdate of the Virgin Mary.
20 April 1949:	*Amethyst* under attack, my first wedding day in 1962

There is a thirteen-year gap between these two dates equalling the number of the first house I moved to after my divorce and significantly the home I have now with my present husband.

25 December 1950:	my husband's birthday, Christmas Day
5 July 1996 2 a.m. in England:	my mother died on Independence Day in America; she fiercely fought for her independence.*
31 December 1998:	I found my Canadian brothers, New Years Eve
6 June 2006 (666):	date of my DNA testing

---

* Due to the time difference, it was still 4 July (Independence Day) in America when she passed away.

25 May 2006:	my first court appearance, Victoria Day in Canada.
9 October 2006:	the final hearing, Thanksgiving in Canada.
12 October 2006:	I received the General Form of Judgement declaring that Leslie Joseph Doyle was my father, my mother's birthday.

On my father's WWII battery photograph taken in Kent, England, the photographer's address is shown as Sydenham, Kent. My eldest brother was later found to live at an address of which Sydenham was a part.

Is there magic in my life or not? As the court order giving permission to have my father's name added to my certificate was dated on my mother's birthday, I consider this a gift from her.

A LETTER TO MY FATHER

Spring 2004

Dear Leslie Doyle,

The thing I wanted most when little was a father to pick me up and carry me on his shoulders like all the other kids seemed to have. I yearned for that.

Now I see the loving relationship my eldest son has with his two daughters and I would not begrudge them that. I am genuinely pleased for them, but I can see what I've missed and it hurts me.

'What can ever make up for that?' I asked the counsellor today, and she said, 'Nothing can'. So how has that helped me? To mourn what I've never had. A brother, a sister, a full-time mum, a father? How does that affect the interaction I have had with others all my life? It feels like being a handicapped person, but no gentle slopes are created for me when I navigate situations. No one comes to help me negotiate the terrain, because you can't see my drawback. People, if they did once see, have forgotten and probably think I should be over that by now, like my first marriage, when people said I couldn't have really loved him because he had people on the side all the time, and was never with me and the children. I got hurt time after time, but I did love him, I would not have married him otherwise, and it does still hurt to have the wounds reopened every day almost by some means or other. I must be extra sensitive but that is how I am. Then to top it all to have the first husband unfaithful many times over and then leave me because I protested at his infidelity. Can one wonder that I have put up with anything to keep the peace rather than stir up more trouble again?

So where does that leave me? I can't blame a father who was one of twelve siblings and the eldest to boot. He was allowed to run wild no doubt and perhaps had no love or attention either. If I look to blame anything I suppose it must be circumstance, maybe one shouldn't try and apportion blame after all. Maybe that is just how it is, I can't believe that I chose this in order to learn life's lessons as some schools of thought suppose.

I dreamed of finding you all my life and when I did catch up with your family, you were freshly laid underneath the ground, passing like ships in the night we were, and you hadn't wanted to see me anyway. I wrote two letters to you. A mediator responded to the first relating that you refused to have contact with me, the second arrived too late. I cannot believe that people can be so heartless as my first husband and my father, what a taste that gave me for a cold cruel world.

Detached and uncompassionate waves move over and through me from the outside world. Would I feel like this if I had had a normal two-up two-down parenting and offspring experience?

Watching it I see so many people even professionals, make promises, or gifts of praise, that they cannot keep and do not remember, the latter being as bad as taking the gift back once you have opened it. How serious is that for someone looking for the best in people!

Did you promise my mum anything at the start? Was she aware this was a fleeting relationship; were you completely honest? One wonders.

Whatever, I still have to come to terms with the loss of a father. My half sister was adopted into a really caring family she says – father, mother, two brothers – bully for her, I would be glad and am secretly, but she needn't exhibit it so often to me.

So there are some really cold people out there Dad and you were one of them. To blazes with everyone else, just please yourself and make hay whilst the sun shines. I for one can't tell what makes those people tick. Is part of you in me? I searched and I can't find it.

From your biological child and namesake,

Lesley.

THE SEARCH FOR MY PAST: A CHRONOLOGY

28 FEBRUARY 2006

I received email advice from the governing body to go to a solicitor and followed their recommendation to go to a register office.

9 MARCH 2006

I went to Crowborough Register Office in my home town to find out how I should go about obtaining a copy of my full birth certificate with the information about my mother and father. I strongly suspected that my father's name would not be displayed on my full birth certificate. I showed the registrar the receipt and short birth certificate I had in my possession and was directed to phone Tunbridge Wells County Court, Kent to enquire further. I returned home and immediately phoned Tunbridge Wells County Court and explained the situation. They directed me to contact a magistrates court of my convenience if, as they also suspected, I needed to take action to acquire my father's name (at the time of my birth, it was unlawful for an unmarried couple to be registered together as parents on a birth certificate).

12 MARCH 2006

The search for the church of my baptism and our nearby former residence of 6 Beblets Cottages, Worlds End Lane, Green Street Green, Farnborough (now incorporated into Orpington), Kent. This is not far from the tiny village of Chelsfield where I was born.

14 MARCH 2006

Looked for Waldens, where I'd lived in July 1946. I was then directed by locals from Chelsfield Village to do unplanned research at Bromley Planning in the Civic Centre Building to find the whereabouts of the original site of Beblets cottages, shown as our place of residence on Mother's ID card from 1944.

After that, I decided to make an unplanned visit to their register office department, sited in the same grounds, to enquire about getting a full birth certificate. I managed to obtain this and discovered the residence and road of my birth place for the first time.

On my way home, I detoured to find the road, but was not able to find the residence. I had, however, confirmation from the birth certificate that my father's name was absent from the document – only my mother and I were registered.

15 MARCH 2006

Letter to Waldens requesting information. Reply from Bromley Planning Department regarding Beblets Cottages.

16 MARCH 2006

Travelled to Maidstone Magistrates Court to apply for the Declaration of Parentage I knew I needed to make in order to have my father added to my first full birth certificate (newly acquired). I filled in forms and returned home to await the outcome, as the court could not be positive as to whether my wish could be fulfilled.

26 MARCH 2006

Received letter from court inviting me to appear for the first time.

28 MARCH 2006

Completed affidavit arrives from Cath.

7 APRIL 2006

Reply from Local Studies Library regarding the location of the house called Elmwood, where I was born, in Chelsfield, Kent.

22 MAY 2006

Tunbridge Wells County Court. At 2.45, I received a directional hearing with a District Judge as it was decided that the matter would be more appropriately dealt with there.

9 OCTOBER 2006

I was given a Final Hearing in Tunbridge Wells County Court at 3 p.m. with yet another judge. The case was listed and heard under the Declaration as to Parentage under Section 56 (1) (a) of the Family Law Act 1986.

I was issued with the General Form of Judgement from Tunbridge Wells County Court stamped on the 12 October 2006, which declared that Leslie Doyle was the parent of the Applicant.

26 APRIL 2007

Applied for Canadian citizenship, the result of which could take eighteen months.

30 JULY 2007

Revisited the town of our two evacuations.

Printed in the United Kingdom
by Lightning Source UK Ltd.
131324UK00001B/229-240/P